Did she dare to hope...?

Yell all you want, she told him silently. I'm not giving up on you, Luke Marino. I'm going to help you whether you want it or not.

"Hey, M.K., catch."

Hearing her brother Gabe's voice, Mary Kate turned to see a bright blue exercise ball heading toward her. Off-balance, she grabbed for it, missing and stumbling toward the wheelchair. Before she could hit it, Luke grabbed her, his strong hands steadying her.

"Sorry," she muttered, straightening herself. "My brother's an idiot at times. I didn't mean to run into you."

"It's okay." His hand still encircled her wrist, his fingers warm and strong. She glanced at him, aware of how close they were, of how dark those smoky eyes of his were. That emotion seemed to dance between them, and she felt sixteen again.

Books by Marta Perry

Love Inspired

A Father's Promise #41
Since You've Been Gone #75
†Desperately Seeking Dad #91
†The Doctor Next Door #104
†Father Most Blessed #128
A Father's Place #153
‡Hunter's Bride #172
‡A Mother's Wish #185
‡A Time To Forgive #193
‡Promise Forever #209
Always in Her Heart #220
The Doctor's Christmas #232
*True Devotion #241

*Hero in Her Heart #249
*Unlikely Hero #287
*Hero Dad #296
*Her Only Hero #313
*Hearts Afire #380
*Restless Hearts #388
*A Soldier's Heart #396

Love Inspired Suspense

In the Enemy's Sights #20
Land's End #24
Tangled Memories #28
Season of Secrets #32

†Hometown Heroes
‡Caldwell Kin
*The Flanagans

MARTA PERRY

has written everything, including Sunday school curriculum, travel articles and magazine stories in her twenty years of writing, but she feels she's found her home in the stories she writes for the Love Inspired Line.

Marta lives in rural Pennsylvania, but she and her husband spend part of each year at their second home in South Carolina. When she's not writing, she's probably visiting her children and her beautiful grandchildren, traveling or relaxing with a good book.

Marta loves hearing from readers, and she'll write back with a signed bookplate or bookmark. Write to her c/o Steeple Hill Books, 233 Broadway, Suite 1001, New York, NY 10279; e-mail her at marta@martaperry.com or visit her on the Web at www.martaperry.com.

A Soldier's Heart

Marta Perry

Steeple Hill®

Published by Steeple Hill Books™

STEEPLE HILL BOOKS

Steeple Hill®

ISBN-13: 978-0-373-81310-0
ISBN-10:   0-373-81310-4

A SOLDIER'S HEART

www.SteepleHill.com

Printed in U.S.A.

The Spirit of the Lord God is upon me, because the Lord has anointed me to preach good tidings to the poor; He has sent me to heal the brokenhearted, to proclaim liberty to the captives, and the opening of the prison to those who are bound; to proclaim the acceptable year of the Lord, and the day of vengeance of our God; to comfort all who mourn, to console those who mourn in Zion, to give them beauty for ashes, the oil of joy for mourning, the garment of praise for the spirit of heaviness; that they may be called trees of righteousness, the planting of the Lord, that He may be glorified.

—*Isaiah* 61:1-3

Chapter One

She was keeping an appointment with a new client, not revisiting a high school crush. Mary Kate Donnelly opened her car door, grabbed the bag that held the physical therapy assessment forms and tried to still the butterflies that seemed to be doing the polka in her midsection.

What were the odds that her first client for the Suffolk Physical Therapy Clinic would be Luke Marino, newly released from the army hospital where he'd been treated since his injury in Iraq? And would the fact of their short-lived romance in the misty past make this easier or harder? She didn't know.

She smoothed down her navy pants and straightened the white polo shirt that bore the SPTC letters on the pocket. As warm as this spring had been, she hadn't worn the matching navy cardigan. The outfit looked new because it *was* new—just as new as she was.

Nonsense. She lectured herself as she walked toward the front stoop of the Craftsman-style bungalow. She was a fully qualified physical therapist and just because she'd chosen to concentrate on marriage and children instead of a career didn't make her less ready to help patients.

The truth was, her dwindling bank balance didn't allow her any second thoughts. She had two children to support. She couldn't let them down.

The grief that was never far from her brushed her mind. Neither she nor Kenny had imagined a situation in which she'd be raising Shawna and Michael by herself. Life was far more unpredictable than she'd ever pictured.

For Luke, too. He probably hadn't expected to return to his mother's house with his legs shattered from a shell and nerve damage so severe it was questionable whether he'd walk normally again.

Ruth Marino's magnolia tree flourished in the corner of the yard, perfuming the air, even though Ruth herself had been gone for nearly a year. Luke had flown from Iraq for the

funeral. Mary Kate had seen him standing
tall and severe in his dress uniform at the
church. They hadn't talked—just a quick
murmur of sympathy, the touch of a handshake—that was all.

Now Luke was back, living in the house
alone. She pressed the button beside the red
front door. Ruth had always planted pots of
flowers on either side of the door, pansies in
early spring, geraniums once the danger of
frost was past. The pots stood empty and
forlorn now.

There was no sound from inside. She
pressed the button again, hearing the bell
chime echoing. Still nothing.

A faint uneasiness touched her. It was
hardly likely that Luke would have gone out.
Rumor had it he hadn't left the house since
he'd arrived, fresh from the army hospital.
That was one reason she was here.

"You went to high school with him." Carl
Dickson, the P.T. center's director, had
frowned at the file in front of him before
giving Mary Kate a doubtful look. "Maybe
you can get him in here for an assessment.
He's refused every therapist we've sent. You
certainly can't do any worse."

She had read between the lines on that.

She was new and part-time, so her hours were less valuable. Dickson didn't want to waste staff on a patient who wouldn't cooperate, but he also didn't want to lose the contract from the U.S. Army if he could help it.

She pressed the bell again and then rapped on the door, her uneasiness deepening to apprehension. What if Luke had fallen? His determination to reject every professional approach, even simple acts of kindness, left him vulnerable.

She grabbed the knob, but it refused to turn under her hand. Kicking the door wouldn't get her inside, tempting as it was, and if Luke lay helpless, he couldn't answer.

She stepped from the stoop and hurried around the side of the house toward the back door. She'd grown up less than two blocks away, in the house where her parents still lived. Luke had been at their place constantly in those days, shooting hoops on the improvised driveway court. A frayed basketball hoop still hung from the Marino garage, mute testimony to Luke's passion for sports.

The back porch had the usual accumulation—a forgotten rake, a trash can, a couple of lawn chairs leaning against the wall. She hurried to the door and peered through the glass at the kitchen.

At first she thought the figure in the wheel-chair was asleep, but Luke roused at her movement, fastening a dark glare on her. He spun the wheels of the chair, but she didn't think he was planning to welcome her in. She opened the door and stepped inside, closing it behind her.

"Don't you wait to be invited?" The words came out in a rough baritone snarl. Luke spun the chair away from her, as if he didn't want to look at her.

Or, more likely, he didn't want her to look at him.

Her throat muscles convulsed, and she knew she couldn't speak in a normal way until she'd gotten control of herself. But Luke—

The Luke she remembered, as a high school football hero, as a police officer, as a soldier when his reserve unit was called up, had been all strength and muscle, with the athletic grace and speed of a cheetah and a relaxed, easy smile. Not this pale, unshaven creature with so much anger radiating from him that it was almost palpable.

She set her bag carefully on the Formica-and-chrome table, buying a few more seconds. She glanced around the kitchen. White-painted cabinets, linoleum on the floor, Cape Cod curtains on the windows— Ruth hadn't changed anything in years.

"I didn't think I had to stand on ceremony with an old friend," she managed to say, her voice gaining strength as she spoke. "Besides, I thought you might not let me in if I waited for an invitation."

He didn't answer the smile she attempted, sparing her only a quick glance before averting his face. "I don't want company, Mary Kate. You must have heard by now that I've made enemies of half the old ladies at church by rejecting their casseroles."

"Mom wouldn't appreciate being called an old lady, so you'd better not repeat that in her hearing."

Her mother had tried, and failed, in her quest to see that Luke had a home-cooked meal delivered by the church every night. Luke had apparently slammed the door in the face of the first volunteer and then refused to answer the bell for anyone else. After a week of refusals, her volunteers had given up.

"I didn't mean—" he began, and then stopped, but for just an instant she'd seen a glimmer of the old Luke before his face tightened. "I don't want visitors."

"Fine." She had to make her voice brisk, or else the pain and pity she felt might come through. She knew instinctively that would only make things worse. "I'm not a visitor. I'm your physical therapist."

He stared for a moment at the crest on her shirt pocket, swiveling the chair toward her. His legs, in navy sweatpants, were lax against the support of the chair.

"Doesn't your clinic have rules against you barging in without an invitation?" Once again the old Luke peeked through in a glimpse of humor.

"Probably." Definitely, and as the newest member of the staff, she couldn't afford to break any of the rules. On the other hand, she couldn't go back and admit failure, either. "Are you going to report me, Luke?"

His dark brows drew down like a slash over deep brown eyes. He'd once been the guy most often talked about in the girls' locker room, mostly because of those eyes. Smoky eyes, with a hint of mystery in them. Combined with the chiseled chin, firm mouth, jet-black hair and the glow of his olive skin, his looks and that faintly dangerous charm had had the girls drooling over him.

And he'd picked her. For a brief time, she'd gone out with the most sought-after guy in school. She hadn't thought of that in years, until today. Seeing him now brought it all flooding back—those days when you were up in the clouds one minute because that special guy had smiled at you and down in the depths the next because he'd smiled at someone else, too.

It hadn't lasted, of course. Maybe, in her naive first love, she'd been too clingy. Luke had made excuses, failed to return phone calls and finally had been seen in the back row of the movie theater with Sally Clemens. She'd given him back his class ring, kept her chin up and done her crying in private.

Luke just stared at her. Maybe he was remembering that, too. Finally, he shook his head, the stubble of his beard dark against the pallor of his skin. "No, I won't turn you in. Just beat it, okay?"

"Sorry, I can't." She pulled out one of the chrome kitchen chairs and sat down, reaching for the forms in her bag. "You're two weeks past due to report to the clinic for your evaluation and therapy. Why?"

His jaw clenched. "I've spent the last three months being poked and prodded by army experts. If they couldn't get me out of this chair, I don't think your outfit can. Just go back to your boss and tell him I appreciate it, but I don't need any more therapy."

His words twisted her heart. What he'd gone through would be horrible for anyone, but for Luke, who'd spent his life relying on his strength and skill on the playing field, then in the military and on the police force—well, this helplessness had to be excruciating.

Showing the pity and compassion that welled up in her was exactly the wrong way to react. To offer him sympathy would be to rub salt into an already agonizing wound.

But she couldn't walk away. He needed her help, or someone's help, whether he wanted it or not.

And she needed to make a success of this. A little flicker of the panic that had visited her too often since Kenny's death touched her. She had to provide financially for her kids, and that meant she had to prove herself at the clinic.

She took a steadying breath. "Sorry, Luke. I'm afraid I can't do that."

"Why not?" He shot the words at her,

swinging the chair closer to her in one fierce movement. "I don't need your therapy and I don't want it. Why can't you just understand that and leave me alone?"

His anger was like a blow. She stiffened in response. She couldn't let him chase her off, the way he had everyone else.

"I can't. And you don't really have a choice, do you? If you continue refusing to cooperate, the army will slap you back into a military hospital. And I don't think they'll let you bully them."

Bullying? Was that really what he was doing? All Luke knew was that he had to get rid of Mary Kate the way he'd gotten rid of everyone else who'd come to the door since he'd returned home.

And of all the people he didn't want to meet while sitting in a wheelchair, Mary Kate Flanagan Donnelly had to be somewhere near the top of the list.

He lifted an eyebrow, trying to find the right attitude to chase her away. "Looks like sweet little Mary Kate learned how to play hardball."

Judging by the annoyed look in those big

blue eyes, she didn't care for that comment, but which part of it she disliked, he wasn't sure.

"It's been a long time since anyone's called me *sweet* and *little,* Luke. Welcome to the twenty-first century."

"Sorry." Funny to be alone with her now. He'd hardly seen her during the years after high school. She'd gone away to college— he'd enlisted in the service. When he'd come back and taken the job with the Suffolk Police Force, she and Kenny were already married, starting a family and moving in completely different circles. And then his reserve unit had been called up and he was gone again, this time to Iraq.

Once, he and Kenny had played football together. He and Mary Kate had dated. Funny to remember that now. They'd all been a lot more innocent then.

"I heard about Kenny." He pushed the words out, a reminder that he wasn't the only person suffering. "I'm sorry."

She paled under those Flanagan freckles, her lips firming as if to hold something back. When she'd walked in the door, slim and quick as the girl she'd been, he'd thought she hadn't changed at all.

Now he saw the differences—in the fine lines around her intensely blue eyes, in the determination that tightened her soft mouth. The hair that had once fallen to her shoulders in bright red curls was shorter now, curling against her neck, and it had darkened to an almost mahogany color.

She gave a curt nod in response to the expression of sympathy, as if she'd heard it all too many times. Well, then, she ought to understand how he felt. No help, no pity. Just leave me alone.

"The kids must be getting pretty big by now. Are they doing all right?" He put the question reluctantly, knowing that old friendship demanded it, knowing, also, that the more he treated her as a friend, the harder it would be to get her to leave.

Her face softened at the mention of her children. "Shawna's eight and Michael is six. Yes, they're doing fine. Just fine."

Something, some faint shadow in her blue eyes, put the lie to that repeated assertion. Tough on kids, to lose their father at that age. At least Kenny hadn't had a choice about leaving, like his father had.

He studied her, drawn out of his own circle of pain for a moment. Mary Kate's hands gripped the pad of forms a bit too tightly, her knuckles white. She still wore a plain gold band on her left hand.

How are you doing, Mary Kate? Really? How it must have pained Kenny to leave her, especially to let her see him dwindling away from cancer. No doubt Kenny would have preferred to go out in a blaze of glory fighting a fire.

Just as he'd rather have been standing a few feet closer to that bomb—to have died quickly and cleanly instead of coming home mutilated.

He glanced from her hands to her face, seeing there the look he dreaded. "I don't want your pity." He ground out the words, because if he didn't he might scream them.

"I'm not pitying you for your injury. I'm just sorry you've come home such a jerk." She leaned toward him. "Come on, Luke, admit it. You're not going to get out of this. The U.S. Army won't release you until they know they've done their best for you. You're lucky they let you come home for the therapy, instead of keeping you in the hospital."

"*Luck* is not a word I associate with this."

He slapped his useless legs, getting a stab of pain in return.

"Fine." Her voice was crisp, as if she'd moved into a professional mode where friendship had nothing to do with them. "We both know I'm right."

He'd like to deny it, but he couldn't. If the army wanted him to have this therapy, he'd have it if they had to drag him kicking and screaming. Not that he could do much kicking.

"Okay." He bit off the word. "When you're right, you're right." At least with Mary Kate, he was over the worst—that moment when she looked at him and saw the ruin he was.

Surprise and relief flooded her face. "That's great." She shuffled the forms, picking up a pen. "We'll send the van for you tomorrow—"

"No."

She blinked. "But you said—"

"I'll do the therapy, but I'm not going anywhere. You can come here." Conviction hardened in him. He wasn't going out where anyone might see him. "And don't bother telling me you don't do that. I know you do in-home therapy."

"That's true, but we have equipment at the center that you don't have here. There's a therapy pool, exercise bikes, weight machines—all the things you might need." She dangled them like a lollipop in front of a recalcitrant child.

"So we'll improvise. That's the deal, M.K. Only you, only here. How about it?"

If she reacted to the high school nickname, she didn't let it show. Obviously she'd toughened up over the years. Still, she had to be easier to deal with than those hard-nosed army docs who'd outranked him.

"I can't authorize something like that."

"Then go back to your boss and get him to authorize it. Deal?"

She must have seen this was the best she could hope for, because she shuffled the papers together and shoved them back in her bag. Her lips were pressed firmly together, as if to hold back further argument.

"I'll try. I can't speak for the director, but I'll tell him what you said."

"Good." Well, not good, but probably the best he was going to get. He watched her hurry to the door, as if afraid he'd change his mind.

He wouldn't. He'd drag himself through whatever torture she devised, because he couldn't get out of it, but in the end it would amount to the same thing. Whether he was in a wheelchair or staggering around like an old man with a walker—either way, his life was over.

The butterflies in her stomach had been replaced by the tightness in her throat that said she'd bitten off a lot more than she could chew. Mary Kate drove down Elm Street toward her parents' house, glancing at her watch. It was too late to catch Mr. Dickson at the clinic. Her revelation of the terms Luke had put on his therapy would have to wait until tomorrow.

How would Dickson react to that? She honestly didn't know her new employer well enough to guess. He might be relieved to have a difficult situation resolved. Or he might think that she had overstepped her bounds and used her friendship with Luke to gain the case for herself instead of persuading him to come to the clinic.

It's not as if I have a choice. You understand that, don't You? I have to take care of the children, so I have to do whatever it takes to succeed at this job.

Sometimes she thought these running conversations with God were all that had kept her going throughout the past year. Even when she'd been venting her anger, raging at the injustice of Kenny's death, she'd been aware of God's daily presence. She might have been furious with Him, but she'd always known He was there.

I'm sorry—I'm thinking too much of myself. Please, be with Luke. Let me be the instrument of Your healing for him.

She pulled into the driveway. Shawna's and Michael's bicycles lay abandoned on the front lawn, but they were nowhere to be seen. She slid out, leaving her bag on the seat, and hurried toward the door. The visit to Luke had taken more time than she'd expected, so her parents had had the children for a longer time after school.

Not that they minded. All the members of her large family were only too eager to help her since Kenny's death. She appreciated it. She just hated needing it.

She walked into the living room. The chintz furniture always looked a little worn and the coffee table bore the scars of the six children who'd been raised here. And now her own two would be here too much, probably, since she'd started work. Her parents deserved to relax in their retirement, not take care of her children.

"Mom?" She crossed to the kitchen, drawn by the aroma of baking chicken. "I'm here." She'd almost said *I'm home,* the phrase the Flanagan kids had always shouted when they rushed in from school or play.

The phrase said that you belonged, that here you were important and valued and sure of your welcome. She thought again of Luke. How must it feel to him to be back in the house where he'd grown up, with his mother gone?

Maybe similar to the way she felt now each time she came here—torn between longing for the reassurance she'd felt as a little girl in this place and feeling as if she ought to be able to handle everything on her own.

"Mary Kate." Her mother straightened from bending over the oven door, pushing the pan back inside. Her cheeks were rosy from the heat and her dark hair curled around her still-youthful face. "You're just in time. Supper will be ready in fifteen minutes. I promised Michael biscuits with the chicken."

Siobhan Flanagan never seemed to look any older—or at least any less beautiful. Why couldn't she have inherited her mother's ageless beauty instead of her father's red hair and freckles?

"You don't need to feed us. We can go home for supper." And have frozen pizza again.

"We want you to stay. Your father and I can't eat all this chicken by ourselves."

She should take the kids, go home, prove to herself that she could manage the whole working-single-mother thing. Still, it was a family joke that after cooking for so many for so long, her mother couldn't fix a meal for two. Twenty, maybe, but not two.

"You spoil us." She'd work on self-reliance tomorrow. "Where are the kids?"

"In the backyard, playing ball. I've been keeping an eye on them from the window."

Shawna and Michael were fine. Of course they were. So what compelled her to step out onto the back porch, just to be sure?

"Hi, Mom." Shawna waved a bright red plastic bat. "Look at the neat ball set Grandpa got for us."

"Very nice."

Michael came running to give her a hug. She held him tightly for an instant, wondering how soon he'd begin to emulate Shawna's independence, making these embraces a thing of the past.

Michael squirmed out of her arms. Looking at his blue eyes and golden red curls was like looking into a mirror. Everyone had always said the kids had little of their daddy in their appearance. That hadn't bothered her too much until Kenny was gone.

"Grandpa says the ball set is ours, but we should leave it here to play with when we're here," Michael said, with his typical determination to do everything according to the rules. "They're our Grandpa's house toys."

"That's a good idea." She ruffled his red curls. "I'm going in the house with Grammy. You two stay right in the yard, okay? If you hit the ball outside, you come and tell me. Don't go after it yourselves."

"We know, Mom." Shawna gave an exaggerated sigh.

Was she being overprotective? Maybe that was inevitable. She'd learned that disaster could strike just when everything seemed fine.

She went back into the kitchen, to find her mother pouring glasses of iced tea. She handed one to Mary Kate. "It's so warm for the first of May that I thought I'd make iced tea. So, tell me. How did it go with Luke? Did he actually let you in the house?"

"Not exactly let me in. I'm afraid I barged in."

Her mother's brow wrinkled. "Brendan thought we should respect his wish to be left alone."

"Brendan doesn't know everything, even if he is a minister." After having been raised with her cousin Brendan, she didn't have quite the same reverent attitude toward their minister that the rest of the congregation did. "Anyway, this was business."

"Poor Luke." Her mother's fund of sympathy was unending. "How did he take it?"

"Not well." She still trembled inside when she thought about that encounter. Had she handled it the right way? Someone with more experience might have done it differently, but at least she'd gotten results. "He finally agreed to the therapy. But he put some conditions on it."

"Conditions?"

She swallowed, trying to ease the tension that tightened her throat. "He'll go through with the therapy, but he insists on home visits. And he'll only do it if I'm his therapist."

Her mother clasped her hand. "That's fine,

Mary Kate. You're a good therapist. He couldn't be in better hands."

"I'm not sure Mr. Dickson will agree with that." She gave a wry smile.

"Then you'll just show him how good you are." Siobhan always had high expectations of her kids, and more often than not, they managed to meet them, maybe feeling they couldn't let her down.

"I hope so, but—"

The back door flew open to allow Shawna and Michael to surge through. "Is it almost time for supper?" Shawna surprised Mary Kate by diving into her arms, face lighting up with a smile. "We're starving!"

"In a minute." Mary Kate hugged her and then opened her arms to include Michael. "Group hug, please."

The feel of those two warm, squirming bodies against hers chased away the doubt she'd been about to express. Of course she could succeed. Fueled by the fierce love she had for her children, she could do anything.

Chapter Two

The silence stretched in the clinic director's office when Mary Kate finished describing her visit with Luke—stretched just like her nerves. She fixed her gaze on Carl Dickson's face, determined not to look at the floor like a kid called into the principal's office.

Dickson had a smooth, expressionless face, rather like an egg. It was the perfect mask for a bureaucrat, impossible to read. Why would someone go into physical therapy, the essence of hands-on helping, and then choose to be an administrator?

He cleared his throat. "Well, Mary Kate, you've brought us to a difficult place."

Her heart sank. He was reacting negatively, probably thinking that she was trying to use her one-time friendship with Luke to grab extra hours of work.

"I don't see what else—" she began, but the telephone rang.

Dickson held up his hand in a stop signal. "One moment, Mary Kate. I should take this."

She subsided. That was another, separate annoyance—Dickson's use of her first name. It had been made clear that he was *Mr. Dickson* to her, and the inequality irked. He was probably about her age, but he was already running the clinic.

He'd also shown that he didn't consider her age an advantage. Most of the other therapists were a good ten years younger than she was. She'd started late, and whether she'd catch up was still up in the air.

She surveyed Dickson's degrees, framed and hung on the wall behind his desk, trying to ignore his phone conversation. The glowing recommendations from the instructors of the refresher courses she'd taken had made him willing to give her the part-time position. If she did well, he'd implied that she'd be considered for a full-time job opening up in September. If not...

Given his reaction to the way she'd

handled Luke Marino, that had begun to look doubtful. Tension tightened her hands on the arms of the chair. She had to provide for the children. Kenny hadn't carried much life insurance—after all, the only way he'd ever thought he'd go was fighting fire, in which case there was a department policy.

Her family wouldn't let them be in need, but providing for her children was her job. She couldn't be a burden to her parents or brothers or sister. As for Kenny's elderly, ailing parents—they must never imagine that Kenny hadn't left her well-provided-for.

Dickson hung up and turned back to her, so she focused on him, steeling herself. But he looked ever so slightly more approachable.

"Well, as I was saying, this is not quite the result I expected, but perhaps we can make it work."

She blinked, sure that was not at all what he'd intended to say. "I tried to convince Mr. Marino that the equipment here would be far better than anything I could provide for home therapy."

"Let's not worry about that. We'll arrange for rental of any necessary equipment and we can spare you to work with him at home as much as needed."

Granted, she was the most expendable of the staff, but still— "Will the army cover the cost of rented equipment?"

"Perhaps, but under the circumstances we don't have to rely totally on the army." He nodded toward the telephone. "That was Marino's father on the line. We've been talking about the situation for several days. He's offered to pick up the tab for anything his son needs that the army won't cover."

That startled her into silence. Certainly Phillip Marino could afford it. Several businesses in Suffolk carried the Marino name, including the largest auto dealership. But his estrangement from his former wife and the son of that marriage was almost as well-known as his car ads.

"I don't know that Luke would agree to that," she said slowly. "He and his father— well, they've never seen much of each other."

"That's hardly our concern." Dickson's voice sharpened. "Our focus must be on what's best for the patient, not on the source of our payment."

He was only too pleased at the prospect of collecting from both the army contract and Phillip Marino. She closed her lips firmly. It was not her place to criticize his decisions.

At least this meant that she had a job to do and a chance to prove herself.

Dickson rose, signaling the end of the conversation. "Meet with the senior therapist and draw up a treatment program and a list of the necessary equipment. You have my authorization to put in whatever extra hours are needed. All right?"

She stood, as well. "Of course."

What else could she say? But she was uneasily aware that she was being manipulated from both sides.

Dickson thought he could use her to collect from both the army and Luke's father. And Luke thought he could use her to skate through the mandated therapy with as little effort as possible.

She wasn't sure which she disliked more.

"That's as far as it will go." Luke managed the words through gritted teeth, trying not to sound like a wimp.

Mary Kate, kneeling on the living-room floor next to his mat, just shook her head and continued to press his leg up with both hands. Those small hands of hers were a lot stronger than he'd have expected. The dead weight of his leg had to be a strain, but she hadn't lost that serene expression throughout the whole torturous hour.

He clenched his fists against the mat. "I can't do it."

"Sure you can." Her tone was as gentle and reassuring as if he were a preschooler learning how to tie his shoes. "Just try a little more. We have to do better than yesterday."

"We?" He grunted the word. "I'm the one doing all the work."

That wasn't true. He knew it, but he wasn't about to admit that she'd been struggling as hard as he was to shove him through the exercises, with him arguing all the way.

Well, he had a right to complain. He hadn't asked for this. He didn't want it. Mary Kate would have to accept the bad temper that went with forcing a man to do something he didn't want to do.

Something that hurt. His leg, protesting, stretched a bit farther and he couldn't control the groan that escaped.

"Very good." Mary Kate eased off immediately, bringing his leg back down and massaging it with long, smooth strokes that soothed away the pain. "You went a good half inch farther today than yesterday."

He lay back on the mat Mary Kate had brought with her. Three times they'd done this, and three times she'd pushed him more than he'd have thought possible. Maybe he'd been wrong about Mary Kate being easier to manipulate than the staff at the army hospital. She was quieter, but there was iron beneath her soft exterior. He wasn't sure what he'd expected of a grown-up Mary Kate, but she certainly wasn't the gentle girl she'd been.

He turned his head far enough to look at the waiting wheelchair. It might as well be forty feet high, for the effort it would take to get back into it.

"Quite a climb," she said, guessing his thoughts with uncanny accuracy.

He grunted in agreement. "Hard to believe I used to climb mountains for fun."

He'd loved the adrenaline rush of pushing his body to the utmost as he scaled a sheer rock face, the euphoria of reaching the top and knowing he'd conquered it. Now he couldn't even get himself into a chair.

"Just rest a few minutes." Mary Kate sat back on her heels as if she could use the rest, too. Her hair clung in damp ringlets to her neck, and while he watched she stretched her arms overhead as if trying to relieve taut muscles.

Her willingness to wait for him made him perversely eager to get back into the chair. "Let's do it." He shoved himself up onto his elbows. "No sense in wasting the day lying around."

"Eager to get back to daytime television?" She maneuvered the chair into position and locked the brake before squatting down next to him.

"Not much else to do." He'd been mildly embarrassed when she'd come in and found him watching reruns of sixties comedies.

"Let your friends come by and see you," she said promptly. "Check some books out of the library. Take up a hobby."

"Stamp collecting?" He let her pull his arm across her shoulders. Once he'd have enjoyed being that close to her. Now it just reminded him of his own helplessness.

"You still have a woodworking shop in the room behind the kitchen. I notice your mother never cleared that out."

"No, thanks."

It had been his father's shop originally, not his. He'd hung around, watching, until his father finally saw his interest and showed him how to cut a curve and sand down an edge. After his dad left, he'd kept up with it for a while, maybe out of some stupid belief that his dad would come back and be proud of what he'd made. He'd learned, eventually. He hadn't bothered with it in years.

Mary Kate double-checked the chair's position, and he felt her muscles tighten. "Ready?"

"Ready."

Together they managed to haul his useless body into the chair, but by the time he was settled they were both breathless.

"Good work," she said.

He shoved her hands away, hating that he had to rely on her strength instead of his own. "Don't patronize me. I'm not one of your kids."

A flicker of anger touched her eyes and was gone. "I don't patronize my kids."

So he could hurt her. Disgust filled him. What kind of a man was he? He didn't want her pity, but he also didn't like feeling that she was unaffected. So he sniped at her. Not very pretty, was it?

Mary Kate straightened, seeming to throw off her reactions. "Let's talk about where we're going to put all the equipment that's coming on Saturday."

He shrugged. "I don't care. You decide."

She walked through the archway to the dining room. "I was thinking we might use this room. All we'd have to move out are the chairs and table. The sideboard wouldn't be in the way."

He wheeled after her into the room, his attention caught in spite of himself. "I guess that would work. I'm not likely to be hosting any dinners for eight."

"Or even one, judging by the condition of your refrigerator."

"Just stay out of my refrigerator," he said, knowing she was right. He was subsisting on peanut butter and jelly sandwiches, for the most part.

"Where do you plan to put the table and chairs?" He wouldn't sell the dining-room furniture his mother had kept polished and shining.

Mary Kate touched the smooth surface. "I think it'll be okay in the garage."

"How do you plan to get it there?" He slapped the arms of the wheelchair. "I'm not exactly in shape to move furniture."

"My brothers offered to—"

"No." He cut her off before she could

finish the offer of charity. "Hire someone to do it. I'll pay."

He felt her gaze on him, but refused to return it. He wasn't going to have guys he'd played football and basketball with coming in here, trying to make polite conversation and avoid looking at his wheelchair. Or worse, telling him how sorry they were while they stood there on two good feet.

"Fine." She gave in quickly.

He glanced around the room, picturing it filled with exercise equipment. "Are you sure this equipment rental is going to be covered? I don't want to be presented with a big bill for stuff I didn't want to begin with."

She turned away, seeming to mentally measure the room for the equipment. "It'll be covered," she said shortly. "One thing—we might have to let your car sit out once we put the furniture in the garage."

He shrugged. "Doesn't matter. I ought to sell it, anyway. I won't be driving again."

"You don't know that." She swung toward him, her eyes darkening with concern. "Luke, you can't just give up on things. Nobody can tell how much you're going to recover."

"Nobody?" Anger surged through him suddenly—at her, at God, at himself for surviving. "I can, Mary Kate. I can tell you exactly how much I'm going to recover. Do you want to know?"

She took a step back, as if alarmed by his anger. He should stop, but he couldn't.

"I'm going to be in this chair forever, and nothing you or anyone else does is going to change that."

What was she going to do about Luke? The question revolved in Mary Kate's mind like a hamster on a wheel as she cleaned up the kitchen that evening after supper. The children's voices rose and fell from the living room, where they were engaged in a board game. A game that seemed to involve argument, by the sound of things.

She frowned at the raspberry jelly that had dried on the bottom rung of one of the pine kitchen chairs. It was beyond her understanding how the three of them could make such a mess in the house when they were gone most of the day. It would be summer vacation in a month, and how she'd manage then, she couldn't imagine.

Just like she couldn't see what to do about Luke. The depth of his bitterness continued to shock her. She knew as well as anyone the important role played by the patient's attitude in healing. Luke's anger and isolation would poison any chance of wholeness if someone didn't do something to change it.

And, it seemed, either through chance or perhaps through God's working, that she was the one who was in a position to change that.

Did You put me in this situation? You must have a reason, but I don't see it. Seems to me I'm that last person who can help him deal with loss. I'm still struggling with that myself.

She wouldn't change Luke by encouraging him with words. His irritation when he felt she spoke to him as she'd speak to her children was proof of that.

And speaking of her children, the noise level in the other room had risen dramatically, followed by the clatter of a game board being upset. She tossed the dishcloth into the sink and stalked into the living room, trying to get a handle on her impatience.

"Hey, what's going on in here? Who threw the checkerboard?"

She knew the answer to that without asking. Shawna, who never lost control, looked smug, while Michael's eyes were suspiciously bright. He folded his arms across his chest, his lower lip jutting out.

This didn't look like the right time for scolding. In fact, this wasn't usually her time at all. Kenny had always taken the evening chores with the kids when he'd been off duty. This had been his time to play with them, roughhousing on the carpet despite her protests and supervising baths and bedtime.

She'd scolded him once, when the rough-housing had led to a broken lamp and Michael was in tears over her reaction.

"Let it go." She could almost hear Kenny's voice, soft and steady. "A broken heart is worth crying about, M.K. Not a broken lamp."

Now she had the broken heart, too, but she wouldn't cry. Not in front of the children. Their world had been torn apart by their father's death. She didn't want to make them afraid by letting them see fear or grief in her.

She sat down on the rug, pulling them close to her. "Forget about the game. Tell me about school today. How was it?"

She happened to be looking at Shawna's face when she asked the question, and she saw the quick flicker of hurt in her eyes. She blinked, and it was gone. She stroked the red curls away from her daughter's heart-shaped face.

"Shawnie? Is anything wrong?"

"Everything's okay, Mom."

Michael wiggled, as if he'd say something, but Shawna shot him a look and he stopped.

"Are you sure?" She didn't want to give her children the third degree, but something had dimmed Shawna's brightness for a moment.

"I'm sure." She smiled. "I got a perfect score on my spelling test."

"That's great." She hugged her, storing away the sense of something wrong to think about later. "What did you do at Grammy and Grandpa's?"

"We had a snack," Michael said. "And then we played outside, and Grandpa played ball with us for a while and then we practiced riding our bikes."

"Did you stay right where Grandpa told you to?"

"Yes, Mommy." That was accompanied by a huge sigh. "We always do."

Ridiculous, to worry about them when they were in Mom and Dad's care. And that neighborhood was certainly safe enough—still the kind of place where everyone knew everyone else and looked out for them. Even so, she couldn't seem to stop.

Don't worry. Pray. Mom had a small

plaque with those words hanging in her bedroom. With six kids to raise, she'd probably done plenty of both.

"Well, shall we read a couple of chapters in our book?" They'd been working their way through some of the children's classics, and even Shawna, already reading well, seemed to enjoy being read to.

"Not now, Mommy. Now we want to hear about the soldier." Michael snuggled against her.

"Soldier?" she repeated blankly. "Do we have a book about a soldier?"

"Lieutenant Marino," Shawna corrected. "We want to hear about him. Did you know that he's on our bulletin board at school? And that he got medals?"

She should have realized. The children's elementary school had taken on a project of supporting local people who were serving in the military. Naturally Luke would be included.

Her heart clutched as she thought about Luke now, in a wheelchair. How did you tell children about the terrible cost of war?

"He wrote a letter to me," Michael said.

"He did not!" Shawna, who'd been leaning against Mary Kate, shot upright. "That's a big fib."

"It is not. He did write to me. He wrote a letter and it said 'To Ms. Sumter's boys and girls.' And I'm one of Ms. Sumter's boys, so he wrote to me." His face was very red.

"Of course," she soothed. "He meant his letter for each one of you."

"Well, I don't think—" Shawna began, but subsided at a glance from her mother. "We want to know about him. Is he very hurt?"

She'd always tried to tell them the truth, even when she had to simplify it for them. "He was hurt when a bomb went off near where he was working. It hurt his legs badly."

"Did they have to cut them off?" Michael asked in a matter-of-fact tone.

She squeezed him, wondering where some of his ideas came from. "No, they didn't, but his legs don't work very well yet. That's why I have to help him, to teach his legs how to work again."

"But what if they don't get better?" His little face puckered up.

"They will." She said it with all the sureness she could muster. *If I can help it, they will.*

Maybe it was time for a distraction. She tickled Michael's chin, and he giggled. "You didn't tell me what you did in school today."

He shrugged, turning away, the laughter

vanishing. "We worked on the model town today, that's all."

"I see."

She saw only too well. The model of the city of Suffolk was a tradition for the first-grade classes and the children worked on it all year. When Shawna had been in first grade, Kenny had helped her make a model car for the display. Michael had been so excited about it that Kenny had started one with him. Shortly after that, Kenny was diagnosed.

Two months later he'd been gone. How could it happen that fast? Somehow one always thought of cancer as a long, slow battle. Not this time. They'd never finished the car.

She hugged him. "Listen, would you like me to help you make something for the display?" Her carpentry talents were limited, but maybe she could get a kit.

"No, thank you, Mommy." His politeness was heartbreaking. "Do you think we could go with you someday and meet the soldier?"

"I'm afraid not, honey. He's been sick and he doesn't want any company."

"Maybe when he's better," he said.

"Maybe." She could just imagine Luke's reaction if she turned up one day with her children in tow.

Still, seeing someone besides her might be a good idea. Not the children—that was too chancy. But if the idea that was flickering at the back of her mind worked out, maybe she could push Luke into seeing a couple of his old friends, whether he thought he wanted to or not.

Chapter Three

Luke shoved the pillow out of the way and levered himself onto his elbows to look at the bedside clock. Nearly nine. He had to get up. Today the exercise equipment was arriving, along with Mary Kate and some helpers to move the dining-room furniture. It would be the busiest time this place had seen since he'd come home, thanks to Mary Kate's persistence.

Of course, he could try hiding in his bedroom until they'd been and gone. Let M.K. take care of all of it. But if he did, it would be like her to barge into his bedroom and find him in his pajamas, unshaven. He hadn't let her catch him looking that bad since the first day. He had a little pride, after all. He'd get up.

He swung his legs over the side of the bed, helping them with his hands, and pulled the wheelchair closer. Mary Kate probably wouldn't be fazed at all by finding him in bed. After all, her specialty had always been helping every lame duck who crossed her path.

And now he was the lame duck, wasn't he? Gritting his teeth, he maneuvered the switch from bed to chair, faintly surprised that it seemed a little easier than it had a few days ago.

That warm, nurturing spirit of Mary Kate's had probably been come by naturally. From what he remembered, her mother was exactly the same. And Mary Kate, the oldest of the Flanagan brood, had mothered the rest of them unmercifully.

His mind drifted through those growing-up years as he got ready to face the day. He'd been buddies with Gabe, a year younger than he and Mary Kate, and to some extent with the next younger brother, Seth. Sports had done it. The three of them had been involved in every athletic activity Suffolk High offered.

Even his brief romance with Mary Kate and their breakup hadn't interfered with that friendship. Obviously Mary Kate hadn't bad-mouthed him to her brothers, or that would have meant the end. The Flanagan boys were notorious for protecting their sisters.

Had Mary Kate needed protecting from him? She wouldn't have thought so. In her eyes, she was the one who took care of everybody else. Still, he'd hurt her. He knew it and she knew it, even if she'd never told anyone else.

A lifetime ago. He tossed a damp towel in the general direction of the rack and wheeled his way out toward the kitchen. Mary Kate probably never thought of those days. Her life was too full for trips down memory lane, with a job and two kids to take care of.

As for him—he was just a job to her, and that was for the best. Even friendship required more than he had to offer now.

The doorbell rang, followed by the sound of the door opening. Mary Kate, obviously. She'd insisted on having a key in case of emergency, and he hadn't had the energy to argue with her about it.

He swiveled into the living room and stopped dead. It was Mary Kate all right, but the two men with her weren't the anonymous hired strangers he'd expected. Seth and Gabe Flanagan seemed to fill the room, and at Gabe's heels was a big yellow Lab.

Anger at Mary Kate surged through him. He glared at her, and she looked back with a coolly confrontational stare that dared him to make a scene.

Dared him, and won. He'd felt free to vent his anger on Mary Kate when she'd come in uninvited, but he couldn't seem to do the same to Gabe and Seth. Did that say something about him, or about their relationship?

For a moment no one moved, and then Gabe came forward with his hand extended. "Luke, it's good to see you again."

"Gabe. Seth." At least his handshake was as strong as ever. "I'm surprised to see you. I thought Mary Kate was hiring someone to do this chore."

Seth grinned. "You know our sister. Never pay somebody else to do something if you can talk a brother into handling it."

"We're glad to do it." Gabe ruffled the dog's ears absently as he spoke. "How are you doing?"

His throat tightened, but he forced himself to speak normally. He patted the arm of the chair. "I guess you can see. And you guys? Either of you make captain yet?" Flanagans went into the fire service, everyone knew that.

"Seth's a brigade chief." Gabe nudged his

brother with his elbow. "To say nothing of a husband and father—one little boy and another one on the way."

"Congratulations." Hard to picture steady, easygoing Seth being in charge. He'd always been the quiet one among the Flanagan boys. "What about you?" He glanced at Gabe. "You letting your brother boss you around now on the job?"

Gabe smiled slightly, shaking his head. "I got pretty broken up fighting fire. I guess it was after your reserve unit was called up, so maybe you didn't hear. Left me with seizures, so I wasn't much good on the fire line." He stroked the dog's head. "Max here is a seizure-alert dog."

For a moment he couldn't say anything. Mary Kate might have told him before she brought her brothers in here.

"Sorry." He should say more, but he couldn't seem to think of anything.

Gabe shrugged. "There's more to life than firefighting, but don't tell my dad I said so." He turned to Mary Kate. "Okay, let's get at it. Show us this furniture we're supposed to be moving."

They trooped off to the dining room, and he heard the scrape of chairs. In a moment

Seth and Gabe came back, carrying the table between them, with Mary Kate rushing ahead to open the door. He could hear Seth ribbing Gabe about holding up his end as they went.

Mary Kate came back in. He planted his hands on the chair arms, so annoyed with her he didn't know where to start. "I told you to hire someone."

She shrugged, looking ridiculously like the girl she'd been at sixteen in faded jeans and a navy T-shirt emblazoned with the Suffolk YMCA logo. "You heard Seth. I hate paying for something I can get free."

"This wasn't about money. You just wanted to get them in here. I suppose that business about Gabe was meant to be a lesson to me." Even through his annoyance, he had a sneaking suspicion that sounded petty.

Mary Kate held his gaze for a long moment. "Only if you need one," she said, and walked out.

He sat staring at the kitchen door. Through its window he could see her cross the yard to her brothers, apparently giving them directions about the table. All three disappeared into the garage.

Maybe that was just as well. She'd left him with nothing to say.

A sound had him turning back toward the front door. Two kids stood there staring at him, and with that curly red hair, blue eyes and freckles, it didn't take a genius to figure out that they must be Mary Kate's.

He froze, hands gripping the chair, fresh anger welling. Bad enough that she'd brought her brothers here—it was worse that she'd brought her kids to stare at him.

He tried to moderate the scowl he knew he must be wearing. He might be annoyed, but he wasn't about to scare little children if he could help it. "Are you two looking for your mother? She's out back."

Please, just go out there and find her and stop staring at me.

The girl shook her head and took a step backward. The little boy walked right up to him and put his hand on Luke's arm. "Are you the soldier?"

Are you the soldier? The words echoed loudly in his head, pounding against his skull.

Not anymore. He fought back the urge to say the words out loud. Not when I'm here, helpless, while the men I'm responsible for are still in the line of fire.

* * *

Mary Kate stepped into the kitchen and stopped dead, looking through the archway to the living room—at her kids, standing there next to Luke's wheelchair. Talking to him, with Michael leaning against his knee as if they were old friends.

She fairly flew across the kitchen and into the living room. "Shawna and Michael Donnelly! What are you doing here? You're supposed to be at Grammy and Grandpa's house."

Shawna pressed her lips together, looking guilty. Michael turned an expression of blue-eyed innocence on her.

"We were, Mommy."

"You're not now." She couldn't look at Luke, and she was sure her cheeks were bright with embarrassment. "Who told you that you could come here?"

"Grammy said we could walk to Timmy Nelson's house to play on the swings." Shawna found her voice. "We do that lots of times. We stay right on the sidewalk and walk around the block and we don't cross any streets."

True, they were allowed to walk to the Nelson place. Mary Kate frowned. "This is not Timmy's house."

"Timmy wasn't home," Michael said. "And you said you were going to come here and it was only a little bit farther to walk and we wanted to meet the soldier."

"Lieutenant Marino," Shawna corrected.

She sent a quick glance toward Luke. He didn't look happy, but neither did he look outraged, which he had every right to be.

"And you're here, Mommy," Michael added.

"You were not invited." Neither were Gabe and Seth, of course, but that was beside the point.

"Lieutenant Marino doesn't care," Michael said. "I was telling him about the letter we got. How everybody liked it. He said that was good."

At least Luke hadn't let the children know how he felt about this influx of company. He was undoubtedly saving that for her.

"You should not have come here if Grammy thinks you're at Timmy's. What if she goes there and no one's home? She'll be worried." She snatched the cell phone from her pocket and handed it to Shawna. "Go out to the kitchen, both of you, and wait there for me. Shawna, call Grammy and let her know where you are. Tell her you'll come back with me."

"Yes, Mommy." Shawna turned to Luke. "I'm sorry we came when we weren't invited."

Luke's face wore an interesting expression—he was obviously not used to dealing with children. "That's all right," he mumbled.

"Goodbye." Michael patted his arm. "I hope you feel better soon."

"Thank you." Luke's lips actually twitched, she was sure, before he got them under control.

Once the kids were more or less out of sight, she turned to Luke. "I'm sorry—" she began, but the rumble of a truck pulling into the driveway interrupted her. "The equipment is here," she said quickly. "I'll go and tell them where to put it."

She hurried outside, relieved to have the inevitable confrontation with Luke put off at least for a few more minutes.

Actually, the interruption stretched even longer as her brothers carried out the rest of the chairs and then helped haul the exercise equipment in. The house seemed to rattle with the tread of heavy feet and the good-humored banter of men moving equipment.

She looked around for Luke, to find him sitting in the archway where he could see what was going on. That was encouraging. At least he wasn't hiding himself away.

Gabe paused to say something to him, and Luke replied almost easily, as if they'd been talking together every day. Max pressed close to Gabe's side, as always, and Luke reached out to stroke the golden fur. Something that had been very tense inside her started to relax. Did she dare to hope that this encounter might ease the isolation he seemed determined upon?

She crossed toward them. "Gabe, can you help get the parallel bars in place? I think they should go here, and you'll have to fasten them in place."

She gestured to a spot in the center of the floor. Fortunately there were good solid hardwood floors in here, not carpets for Luke to trip on.

"Parallel bars?" Luke's brows lifted. "Are you planning to turn me into a gymnast?"

"No, I'm planning to help you walk again." She held her breath, waiting for the inevitable explosion.

It didn't come. The black look told her, though, that he was probably just delaying it until they were alone.

Yell all you want, she told him silently. *I'm*

*not giving up on you, Luke Marino. I'm
going to help you whether you want it or not.*

"Hey, M.K., catch."

Mary Kate turned to see a bright blue
exercise ball heading toward her from Seth.
Off balance, she grabbed for it, missing and
stumbling toward the chair. Before she could
land, Luke grabbed her, his strong hands
steadying her.

"Sorry," she muttered, straightening
herself. "My brother's an idiot sometimes. I
didn't mean to run into you."

"It's okay." His hand still encircled her
wrist, his fingers warm and strong.

She glanced at him, aware of how close
they were, of how dark his smoky eyes were.
Awareness seemed to dance between them,
and she felt sixteen again. She tried to find
something to say, and she couldn't think of
a single thing.

Mary Kate looked around the long table at
her parents' house, savoring the moment.
Sunday dinners were a tradition in the
Flanagan family, and at first, after Kenny's
death, she'd found it hard to come alone with
the children. Now that the sharpest pain had
faded, she was back to enjoying these times,

with their reminder of the strength of family bonds. They were fortunate, more so than many families, that life had settled all of them in this area.

She especially loved this moment, when the meal was over. The children had run out into the backyard to play and the adults lingered over their coffee cups, reluctant to break the low rumble of conversation and the precious circle of fellowship.

Gabe's wife, Nolie, leaned forward to pour a little more coffee. "If this nice weather keeps up, we can start doing Sunday picnics out at the farm again."

Gabe held his cup out for a refill. "That means I'll have to paint the porch and put up the swing." He turned toward Mary Kate. "Do you think there's any chance we could get Luke out for one of our picnics? It might do him good."

"There are a lot of things that would help him. Getting him past wanting to hide is the tough part." That occupied her mind whenever she wasn't busy with something else— what could she do to give Luke an interest in life again?

"Poor boy." Her mother's warmhearted sympathy flowed out like a never-failing spring. "If only he wouldn't shut people out. Everyone wants to help."

"Luke always had that independent streak." Gabe seemed to look back through the years. "Even on the football field, he wouldn't wait for anyone to cover him. He'd just charge in and rely on himself. And he was strong enough that nine times out of ten, it worked."

That was Luke, all right. If only she could find a way to turn that tenacity and strength to her advantage in helping him heal— "What happened the tenth time?"

Gabe smiled. "He got pounded into the turf, of course. He always shook it off and jumped up again, grinning like it was fun."

"That's where he is right now. But this time he's not shaking it off."

The other end of the table had gotten into a noisy conversation about baseball, so she lowered her voice to continue with Gabe and Nolie. They were the two people in the family who could most understand what Luke was going through. Gabe, because of his own injury, and Nolie, because she'd helped him accept and overcome.

"It's tough, believe me." Gabe's hand dropped to stroke Max's head. The seizures came very seldom now, but often enough that he still needed Max beside him. "Luke's always relied on his physical strength, and now that's let him down. It takes some getting used to."

"And we don't know what happened to him over there." Nolie was the quiet one in the noisy Flanagan gatherings, but when she spoke, she invariably had something helpful to say. "There could be other things complicating the situation. When it comes to a previously able-bodied person accepting a disability, the emotional is always as important as the physical."

"If you—" she began, but the clinking of a glass distracted her. She glanced to the other end of the table, where her cousin Brendan tapped a spoon against his coffee cup.

"Attention, please." Brendan had shed the clerical garb he'd worn this morning, and his eyes were bright with suppressed excitement. "Claire and I have an announcement to make." He glanced toward his wife, sitting beside him, and Claire's face glowed with love.

In the sudden silence, Mary Kate could hear the quick intake of breath from her mother. Was it the thing they'd all hoped and prayed for?

Brendan reached over to clasp his wife's hand. "We're expecting a baby in November."

The table erupted in joyful celebration, and Mary Kate shoved her worries about Luke to the back of her mind. Her throat went tight with tears as she hurried around the table to hug both of them. Everyone knew they'd been trying to get pregnant for well over a year without success, but now it was finally happening.

She hugged and kissed them, heart full, surprised to find that her joy was tinged with a little sorrow. Self-pity? She hoped not. Still, even though she and Kenny hadn't intended to have more children, she couldn't stem the wave of regret for what would never be.

She glanced at her watch. "Goodness, look at the time." She dashed away a single tear, hoping it would be interpreted as joy for Brendan and Claire. "I'd better check on the kids."

Before she could betray any other emotion, she went quickly through the kitchen. She didn't want anyone to feel they had to mute their celebration because of her loss. Pushing open the back door, she glanced around the fenced-in yard, counting heads.

Shawna played ring-around-the-rosy with the smaller ones: Gabe and Nolie's little Siobhan, Seth and Julie's Davy, Ryan and Laura's Amanda. Michael—

"Shawnie, where's Michael?"

Shawna looked up from the tangle of little bodies on the ground. "I don't know, Mom. He was here a minute ago."

Her heart seemed to skip a beat. "Michael? Michael!" From the bottom of the steps, the whole yard was in view. No Michael.

The door behind her opened and her mother came out, carrying Mary Kate's bag. "Your cell phone is ringing."

She grabbed the bag, yanking the phone out. Michael—

"Mary Kate?" Luke's deep voice grated in her ear. "Your boy is over here. You want to come and get him?"

Chapter Four

Mary Kate realized she was shaking inside as she started the car, and she took a deep breath, trying to still the rush of panic. Michael was all right. Luke would keep him safe until she got there. It was okay.

No, it wasn't. If Kenny were here, he'd have found something to make her laugh in this situation, and his steady, even calm would convince her this wasn't the worst thing that could have happened.

But Kenny wasn't here, and Michael had done the unthinkable, leaving his grandparents' yard without a word to anyone. What on earth had made him do that?

Lord, thank You for keeping him safe. Maybe I'm overreacting—I don't know. I just know that I'm scared and I need guidance.

Please, show me the right way to respond to this situation, with both Michael and Luke.

The short drive around the block to Luke's house wasn't long enough to settle her entirely, but then, she probably wouldn't calm down until she had her son in her arms again. She parked in the driveway and ran to the front door, tapping and then hurrying inside.

"Michael Donnelly." She grabbed him, pulling him against her with an urgent need to know he was in one piece. "Are you okay?"

"Sure, Mommy." He squirmed free. "I'm sorry. I guess you're mad at me, huh?" He gave her the angelic look that said he couldn't possibly have done anything wrong.

She hardened her heart. "Sorry doesn't quite cover it, young man. And don't bother looking at me that way, because you're still going to be punished."

"Your mom's one tough lady, Michael. She doesn't let me get away with anything, either." Luke actually sounded as if he found this amusing—probably because it put her in the position of having to apologize for her children. Again.

She looked at him, praying she wasn't blushing. That was the trouble with fair skin and freckles—every emotion showed. "I'm very sorry Michael bothered you. That shouldn't have happened."

And it won't, ever again, she vowed.

A rare smile crossed Luke's face, chasing away the lines of pain and anger. "He's not a bother. But I knew you'd be worried."

"That's nice of you to say."

And yet she was sure he'd been fit to be tied when he'd called her. Apparently Michael had been exercising his charm during the time it had taken her to drive over.

"I'm sorry if I was a pest," Michael told him. "I didn't mean to be. I just wanted to talk to you."

Why? She wanted to ask the question out loud, but not here, not in front of Luke. She'd have to wait until they were alone for that.

"You weren't a pest," Luke said. He reached out to ruffle the red curls. "But you should never come here without your mom's permission. You know that, don't you?"

"Can I come if she gives permission?" he said promptly.

"Michael." Her mother could always put a wealth of meaning into just saying one of her kids' names. Mary Kate could only hope she'd mastered the trick.

Luke shot her a glance, and then he nodded gravely. "If your mother gives you permission, you can come and see me again. But never go anywhere without permission from the person who's in charge. A soldier who did that would be going AWOL."

Michael nodded, looking impressed. "I promise."

"Good." Luke turned the chair, moving toward the small cherry writing desk in the corner. He opened the top drawer and took something out. "I have something for you."

"You don't have to—" she began, but Luke silenced her with the slight shake of his head.

"This is between Michael and me," he said. He held out a small box. "Here."

Michael fumbled with it for a moment and then managed to pop the lid up. "Wow," he said reverently.

She moved so that she could see the contents of the box, and shock zigzagged through her. She took the box from Michael's hands.

"He can't accept this. You can't give these away." She thrust the box toward Luke, but he clutched the arms of the chair, refusing to take it.

"They're mine. I can do what I want with

them." There was a dark undertone to the words, and she wasn't sure what emotion it expressed. Bitterness? Grief?

She looked down. Against a background of black velvet lay three things. Two she recognized immediately—the Purple Heart and the Bronze Star. It took a moment to identify the third as the Iraq Campaign Medal, with its relief in bronze of the country.

She was at a loss to know how to handle this, and it didn't help that Michael was tugging at her arm. She frowned at him. "Stop, Michael."

"But he said—"

"I know what he said, but these are too valuable to give away."

"I can do what I want with them," Luke repeated, his face set.

A wave of anger took her by surprise. How dare he use her son to precipitate a situation like this?

"It's not appropriate for Michael to keep them," she said firmly. "However, if you'd like to lend them for him to take to school for their display about the military, that would be all right."

Luke's dark eyes lifted to her face, and she thought she saw the faintest regret there. "Fine," he said gruffly. "Do that, then."

She nodded and closed the box, handing it to Michael. "Go out to the car and wait for me. And don't open that."

He took it reverently in both hands and scurried for the door, apparently realizing now was not the time for further argument. Her kids seemed to know exactly how far to push her.

When he was gone, she turned back to Luke. "You shouldn't have done that."

"Sorry." He evaded her gaze. "I didn't think about the value. I just thought he might enjoy them."

She shook her head impatiently. "Of course he couldn't keep them. But I meant you. You shouldn't give away something that important. And don't bother telling me they're yours to do what you like with, because I don't buy that."

"They are."

"Of course they're yours, awarded because you served your country honorably and were injured doing it." She thought of the Bronze Star. "And probably did something heroic in the process, if the Bronze Star means what I think it does."

His face tightened again. "I shouldn't have them."

"Why not?" She wanted to shake the stubbornness out of him. "You earned them."

His glare pinned her to the spot with its ferocity. "Because I don't want medals when I'm here, safe, and my guys are still over there in the line of fire. That's why."

"I hear you're working with that young fellow who's just back from Iraq."

Frank Morgan, one of Mary Kate's favorite patients, slowed the pedals of his exercise bike, looking at her with inquiry in his bright blue eyes. With the fresh pink color of his cheeks and those clear eyes, no one would believe Frank was the eighty-three she knew he was.

"Keep pedaling," she said, tapping the handlebars. She glanced around the nearly empty room at the clinic. No one else was working at the exercise bikes and treadmills this early in the morning. "How did you hear that?"

He smiled, smoothing back his ruffle of white hair with one hand while he increased the rotation speed. "Ha, makes you wonder, doesn't it? Truth is, I'm around this place so much, some of those young things act like I'm part of the furniture. Say anything in front of me, they would."

"Well, if you wouldn't insist on trying to take your own storm windows off, you wouldn't have to come in so often. How does your back feel?" She checked her watch. "Can you go another minute?"

"Sure thing. So, how's that boy doing?"

That was the question that kept her awake at night. How was Luke doing? The incident with his medals had made her feel out of her depth. Maybe he needed to be working with a psychologist, not her. She'd seriously considered admitting to her boss that she felt unprepared to deal with Luke's problems. But she could hardly say that to Frank.

"He's coming along."

He nodded. "Can't talk about a patient. I know. I guess I wouldn't want you talking about me to someone else. Still, I have an interest. It's been a long time, but I remember what it was like when I came home from the war."

"Really? Which war?" She signaled him to slow down gradually.

"Which war, she says." He snorted. "The big war, young lady. World War II."

"I didn't realize." She helped him off the bike. "You must have lied about your age to get in, because you're way too young for that. Ready to work on the resistance bands, or do you want to rest a minute?"

"Lied about my age? No such thing, but I thought I'd never turn eighteen. I was mad to get out there with my buddies." He picked up the resistance bands.

One thing she could say about Frank—he never balked at anything she asked him to do, taking each new task as a fresh challenge. Luke could benefit from a little of his attitude.

"Was it difficult when you came back?" she asked casually. Maybe she couldn't talk about Luke to him, but there was no reason she couldn't try to gain some insight.

He grunted. "I'll say it was hard. Mind, I wasn't injured, like your young fellow, but I'd been in a POW camp for nine months— seemed more like nine years, so I wasn't in great shape. Funny how that is. You come back, and it's just what you dreamed about all that time, but it's strange, as well."

"Strange how?" She adjusted his stance, making sure he was using his back correctly.

He frowned, as if trying to find the right words. "I guess it seemed to me nothing should have changed, but when I came back, life had moved on without me. The worst part was just getting out around people again." He chuckled. "Couldn't remember names to save me, even folks like my brother-in-law and my old boss at the gas station."

Luke seemed to remember names, but he had that same reluctance to be around people. No, *reluctance* wasn't a strong enough word. *Aversion,* maybe. "How did you get over it?"

"My wife, bless her." His eyes filled with tears suddenly, but he was smiling. "She went everywhere with me, holding on to my arm like walking with me was the proudest thing she'd ever done. She figured out about the names without me telling her and she'd always say the name if we ran into somebody. And cover for me if I jumped at a backfire or something like that. The good Lord knows I couldn't have done it without her."

She patted his shoulder. "She loved you. She loved doing it."

He nodded. "That's what your young man needs, too. Folks that love him and will help him along, even if he doesn't act like he wants their help."

His words echoed in her heart as she took the bands from his hands. "Good job. That's it for today. Don't go moving any more storm windows, all right?"

He smiled, his cheeks as pink and round as a baby's. "If a man can't do the things he's always done, he feels like less of a man."

"I guess so." Once again, his words resounded. That was what Luke was feeling, knowing he couldn't do the things he'd always done, maybe even afraid to figure out what he could do now. "But I don't want to see you in here with a broken leg next."

"I'll behave. I promise."

"See that you do." Impulsively she gave him a hug. "I wish I could get the two of you together. You'd be good for him."

He nodded, obviously knowing who they'd been talking about the whole time. "You figure out a way to do it, and I'll be there. It's the least I can do, you know?"

She nodded, her throat tight. It was the least she could do, as well, and she wouldn't give up on Luke, no matter what.

If Luke hadn't felt so guilty for putting Mary Kate on the spot with her kid with those medals, he wouldn't allow her to wheel him down a new ramp into his backyard. Come to think of it, maybe this was her idea of payback. He blinked as she pushed him into the May sunshine.

"Okay, I've been out. I'm ready to go back in now."

Mary Kate set the chair's brake. "You try it, and I'll put a stick in your wheel. If you stay in that house any longer, you're going to turn into a mole."

He frowned at the ramp that led from the back porch to ground level. "Are you sure this ramp is covered?"

"It's taken care of," she said shortly, crossing the grass to look at the flower bed his mother had planted along the porch.

He glanced across the yard, feeling as if he were really seeing it for the first time in a long time. The old apple tree still stood in the corner. He'd had a swing hung from a low branch once, and then later a tree house that had probably damaged a limb or two.

"The garage could use a coat of paint. I guess I should have taken care of things better for my mother."

"I remember when you and Gabe and a couple of other guys started a band and practiced there."

That surprised a smile from him. "Until the neighbors complained. We were probably the worst band in the history of garage bands."

"Then it's a good thing Mom found an

excuse when Gabe wanted to move practice to our house." She bent over to pull a handful of weeds. "These irises are going to be blooming soon."

"You're not being paid to garden." Although he had to admit that his mother would be ashamed to see the state of her backyard. It had been easy to ignore as long as he was holed up inside, but now he couldn't. "Grab one of those chairs and come sit down."

For a moment he thought she'd argue, but then she shrugged and did as he said. She picked up a folding lawn chair and carried it over to him, then sat down.

"I could have brought that down for you." He'd have done it automatically when he had two good legs. So why was he neglecting it now, just because of the wheelchair? He still could have managed the light aluminum chair.

"Yes, you could," she agreed, tilting her face to the sun and closing her eyes.

"You didn't have to agree with me. Like I told Michael, you're one tough lady." He was instantly sorry he'd mentioned the boy. She hadn't said anything about her son since the medal incident.

"I'm sure he thinks so." She didn't open her eyes, but her brow furrowed slightly.

"I wish—" he began, and then stopped. "I know you had to punish him for running off without asking permission." *Say it, you jerk. You owe her an apology.* "I'm sorry."

"For what? I'm sure you didn't encourage him to run off."

She opened her eyes then and looked at him. With the wind ruffling her curls, it wasn't hard to picture her as the kid she'd been, and the realization sent an unwelcome wave of tenderness through him.

"No. I didn't." He swallowed his pride. "I mean about the medals. I should have realized offering them to your son was inappropriate. I know it put you in a tough spot."

"Yes, it did."

He steeled himself, sure she was going to pry into his feelings about the honors, but she didn't. Her brow furrowed again, and she shook her head slightly. "Sorry. I know you didn't do it to give me a hard time."

"I guess I didn't know enough about kids to foresee your reaction. Or his. Is he okay with putting them on display?"

She looked cautiously relieved that he was talking normally about the medals. "He's not mad at me, if that's what you mean. After all, he was the hero of the first-grade class when he brought them in. All the children remember your letter, so of course they're impressed."

"They shouldn't be." His voice roughened in spite of himself. He knew, as well as anyone, that he couldn't go back, but that didn't stop him from feeling he'd let his guys down.

She smiled slightly. "Let's just agree to disagree about that. I suppose that's why Michael felt so driven to come and see you." There seemed to be a question in the look she turned on him.

"Hasn't he told you what was so important that he broke the rules to come over here?"

"He's being quiet about it." She ran her fingers through her mahogany curls, her eyes shadowed. "That's not like him. Or at least it's not what he was like before Kenny died."

"It worries you." He had a ridiculous impulse to reach out and put his hand over hers, to offer comfort. "It must be pretty rough."

"It scares me." Her voice lowered almost to a whisper. "Kenny was always so calm— nothing ever ruffled him. He could laugh at me when I was tying myself in knots with worry, and it would make me so mad, but then I'd be laughing, too."

He held his breath, afraid to speak for fear he'd say the wrong thing. It was almost as if Mary Kate were talking to herself. Maybe sitting still and listening to her was all the comfort he could offer. If so, that's what he'd do.

The telephone rang in the kitchen, and she jerked, realization filling her eyes. "I'm sorry." She jumped up and ran for the phone, probably eager to get away from him.

She was back in a moment, holding the cordless phone cautiously. "It's your father. He'd like to talk with you."

His hands gripped the armrests so hard it was a wonder he didn't bend them. "I don't want to talk to him."

"Luke, don't you think you should—"

"No." He bit off the word. He would not explain. His relationship, or lack of one, with his father was none of her business.

She might understand. He could remember sitting on the porch swing at the Flanagan house one evening after walking her home, pouring out all his pain and anger at his father. In any event, she turned and walked back into the house, phone to her ear, probably trying to find some polite way to tell his father that he wouldn't talk to him if he were the last man on earth.

You didn't want us. That was the only thing he'd say to his father. You didn't want us, and now I don't want you.

By the time Mary Kate came back, he'd managed to shove his father back into the dark recesses of his mind. If she brought it up—

But she sat back down as if they hadn't been interrupted. "I've been wanting to talk to you about a change in your therapy," she said.

"What kind of a change?" She was already pushing him to the limit, he'd have said. What else did she have in mind?

"I know you don't want to go to the clinic—"

"I still don't," he said flatly. He'd had it with places like that at the army hospital. He didn't need any more therapists with their professional smiles. At least Mary Kate expressed honest feelings with him, instead of trying to jolly him along. "Look, let's be frank. We both know I'm not going to get out of this chair."

She swung toward him, reaching out to grab both of his hands in hers. "We don't know anything of the kind, Luke Marino, so don't you say that."

"The doctors said—"

"I've read the reports, and they don't say a word about you not walking again. You have significant muscle weakness and nerve damage, but that's why the therapy is important. We have to strengthen those muscles and give the nerves a chance to build new pathways. It can happen. You have to have faith."

It was hard not to be impressed by her passion, but he doubted. Boy, did he doubt. "I know you think holding out that carrot will make me work harder—"

"You need something to make you work harder,"she snapped. "You're a strong man, Luke. It's time you started acting like it."

He pushed her hands away. "What do you suggest?" he asked bitterly. "Wheelchair athletics?"

"It wouldn't hurt, but I don't expect miracles from you." Her smile flickered. "Just take a chance. If you'd come to the clinic, you could use the pool. That would be wonderful for you, but you're too stubborn to even try it for fear someone might see you."

"Mary Kate—" He had a sinking feeling she might be right, but he sure wasn't going to admit that to her. "Tell you what. I'll make a deal with you."

"What kind of deal?"

"I'll go to the pool and try whatever you want, if you promise me I won't run into another person when I'm there."

That should deter her. He should be satisfied that he'd silenced her on the subject. Instead, he felt like a jerk again. What was it with Mary Kate that kept bringing out that feeling?

Chapter Five

Luke poured a mug of coffee and inhaled the aroma. Maybe the coffee would wipe away the last shreds of the dream. He spun toward the kitchen table and set the mug down, not tasted. Ironic, that the dream of running should bother him almost as much as the nightmare of the bomb.

He frowned down at his legs. Running—something else to add to the list of things he wouldn't do again. In the dream he'd run easily, effortlessly. He'd been back in high school again, running on the school track, legs pounding, heart pumping, feeling as if he could go on forever.

Well, nobody over thirty could run with that careless confidence. That attitude belonged to the teenager who hadn't yet figured out that he was mortal.

The sound of a key in the lock brought his head up. Mary Kate here already, apparently. Well, she could just wait until he'd had some breakfast.

He heard her quick, light footsteps coming across the living room, and then she appeared in the doorway, looking so clean and crisp that he was automatically embarrassed at being unshaven.

"Good morning. Are you still having breakfast?"

"I haven't even started." He picked up the mug. "There ought to be a law against being as cheerful as you are first thing in the morning."

"Maybe the answer is that it's not first thing in the morning for me. The kids get up at seven." She opened the refrigerator door and took out a carton of eggs. "Scrambled or fried?"

"I don't want anything. And I don't expect you to cook for me."

She shrugged. "I may as well. Obviously we're not going to get any work done until you've eaten something. And you have to have breakfast if you don't want to collapse in the middle of your exercises."

"I don't collapse." He ground the words out. He'd said he didn't want sympathy, but Mary Kate was carrying this cool, professional detachment to the extreme.

"Scrambled," she said, getting out a bowl. "And toast. I'd fix bacon, but it doesn't look as if you have any."

"I don't suppose it would do any good to keep telling you I don't want you to cook for me."

"No good at all." She gave him that serene smile and began beating the eggs.

"Did anyone ever comment on how bossy you are? Like Kenny, for instance?"

She was pouring the eggs into the pan, turned away from him, but he could see her slim back stiffen. He was being a jerk again. He couldn't seem to stop.

"I didn't have to be bossy with Kenny. He knew the right thing to do and did it."

"Perfect, in other words." That wasn't how he remembered happy-go-lucky Kenny, but maybe he'd grown up after high school.

"Not perfect." She stopped stirring, seeming to look into the past at the risk of letting the eggs burn. "Just…a man of integrity."

It was obvious she considered that high praise, and it left him without anything to say in return. Or at least, without anything he'd regret even more than he already did.

She moved the eggs quickly onto a plate, buttered the toast and added it and set the plate in front of him. "You know, when I was about ten, I found an injured squirrel on my way home from school."

He blinked at the change of subject and looked down at the plate. He could refuse to eat, of course, but the food looked and smelled better than anything he'd managed to fix. He forked fluffy eggs into his mouth.

"What does a squirrel have to do with anything?"

She poured a mug of coffee for herself and slid into the chair opposite him. "Nothing, I suppose. I remember my brothers and my cousin Brendan were with me, but they were all afraid to touch it."

"So you were the heroine."

"Not exactly." She shrugged. "I just thought I should help."

"I suppose you nursed it back to health and then set it free and it waved goodbye with its furry little paw."

"Actually it bit me."

He sputtered on his coffee, unable to resist

a laugh and surprised at how good that felt. "Are you comparing me to a hurt squirrel?"

"I wouldn't dream of it." Her lips stayed firm, but laughter danced in those blue eyes.

"I suppose your brothers and Brendan carted you home." He remembered how they'd stuck together in trouble, even if Gabe and Brendan and Seth sometimes complained about the girls, or about little brother Ryan.

"It gave Seth a chance to practice his fireman's carry." She grinned. "Not exactly comfortable, as I remember. And Ryan ran screaming into the house to alert Mom. The Flanagan family at our noisy worst, I suppose."

"You guys weren't so bad." He loaded strawberry jam onto the toast, wondering where it had come from. This was obviously not the store-bought stuff. "I used to envy all the chaos at your house. It always seemed... welcoming."

His mother's house, with its moody silences and spotless cleanliness, had been the exact opposite of the random, cheerful routine at the Flanagans'. His mother had acted as if an inspector were about to arrive to check things out.

"Believe me, it hasn't changed when we get together. It's even louder, with all the kids now."

He could imagine. "Doesn't it drive your parents crazy?"

"You'd think so, but it must not, since they still try to get us all together for dinner every Sunday. And everyone is still welcome." Her gaze fixed on his face. "Why don't you join us on Sunday? They'd love it."

"No." He wouldn't make an excuse for the abrupt answer. Maybe Mary Kate could make him eat and make him exercise and even make him smile, but she couldn't make him go anywhere.

"Well, that's too bad. Maybe another time." She rose, carrying dishes to the sink. "By the way, I have things arranged at the clinic pool for tomorrow night."

It took a moment for the words to register. He turned the wheelchair slowly, resisting the impulse to slam it around. "Then you can un-arrange them. I told you I wouldn't go."

"Wrong." She swung around, bracing her hands against the counter behind her. "You told me you wouldn't go unless I could guarantee you wouldn't see anyone. You won't."

"That's ridiculous." He could feel the

tension curl inside him at the thought of getting into a car, driving to the clinic, going into a strange place— "You can't possibly guarantee that. I'm not going."

He started to turn away. Mary Kate swooped toward him, grabbing both arms of the chair, her face inches from his, blue eyes blazing.

"No way, Luke Marino. You promised, and I've jumped through more hoops than you could believe to be sure we'll have that area of the clinic totally to ourselves tomorrow night. If you think you can back out now, you'd better think again."

He was too aware of how close she was— close enough that he could catch the faint floral aroma that clung to her, close enough that he could count the dusting of freckles on her smooth cheeks. His heart was pumping, and he didn't think it was just at the prospect of going out in public.

"I don't want to." He suspected he sounded like a sulky kid.

"Too bad." She seemed to become aware of how near they were—he saw it in the faintly startled darkening of her eyes. She straightened, folding her arms across her protectively. "Get used to it. You're going."

* * *

She hadn't been particularly sympathetic to Luke. But maybe tough love was the only thing that was going to get him out of his cocoon and into the world again. Mary Kate pushed a strand of wet hair away from her face and caught the damp towel Michael had been using before it hit the tile floor of the bathroom.

"Towels belong on towel racks, not on the floor." Maybe her kids could use a little of that, too.

Michael shrugged, pouting a bit as if on the verge of talking back, but then he hung up the towel, more or less neatly.

Michael probably realized her supply of patience was dwindling. She handed him his pajamas, resisting the urge to help him put them on. Michael had long since outgrown the need for her help in getting dressed, but sometimes she longed to go back to those baby days, when all the problems were ones she knew how to handle.

She didn't feel confident that she was handling Luke in the right way, although at least he'd stopped arguing and given his grudging consent to the pool idea. And she definitely wasn't sure how to handle this most recent issue with Michael.

"Aunt Nolie stopped by this afternoon." She toweled his curls. Gabe's wife, Nolie, was teaching the first-grade Sunday School class this year, so she had Michael. "She said you got a little upset in class this week."

Actually, what she had said was that Michael had acted up during the Bible story, and that she'd finally had to make him change seats. But it didn't seem fair to either Nolie or Michael to reveal she knew that much.

He shrugged, his face closed to her. Her heart clenched. His expression reminded her of the one Luke so often wore.

"Honey, if something's wrong in church school, you can tell Aunt Nolie. Or you can tell me. You know that, don't you?"

She'd asked Nolie what the story was, hoping for a clue. It had been the one about men lowering their sick friend through the roof of the house so that Jesus could heal him. Pain had shot through her at that, and she'd felt a moment of irrational anger at Nolie. Irrational, because Nolie could hardly avoid mentioning healing.

Michael shrugged. "Nothing's wrong, Mommy." He squirmed away from her. "Can I go get my snack?"

Let me make it better. That was what she

wanted to say. Instead she nodded and tried to smile. "Go ahead."

He rushed off, and she bent over the tub to let the water out, letting a tear or two go with it. Tired, she was so tired, and she'd begun to feel that she wasn't doing anything well anymore—with the kids, with her job—

Lord, why does it have to be so hard? Just when I think I'm coping really well, it hits me, and I feel as if I'm right back where I started, trying to make sense of Kenny's death, trying to figure out how to go on alone....

She straightened, wiping her hands on the towel and frowning at her blurred face in the steamy mirror. *Stop feeling sorry for yourself. It doesn't become you, and it certainly doesn't do any good.*

And she wasn't really alone. Always, no matter how she fumed or wept or doubted, she knew that her Father was there, ready to take her hand. The tightness in her throat dissolved slowly away.

The peal of the doorbell sent her hurrying out to the living room. It couldn't be any of the family—they'd have rapped once and then walked in, calling her name. She swung open the door and froze with words of welcome drying on her tongue. It was Luke's father, Phillip Marino.

"Mrs. Donnelly." He smiled, but she could read tension in the way he stood there—shoulders stiff, hands clenched. "May I come in? I'd like to talk with you."

Professional rectitude rushed to her aid. "I'm sorry, Mr. Marino, but I can't discuss a patient with anyone." That was what had brought him to her door, of course. Luke—his son, her patient.

"No, no, of course I realize you can't divulge any medical details, but—" He paused, glancing over his shoulder at the quiet residential street. "May I come in, please? I won't take much of your time."

She could hardly refuse, even though warning bells were going off in her mind. She stepped back, gesturing him in. "Just for a moment, then. I'm getting my children ready for bed."

Closing the door behind him, she realized said children were standing in the living room, staring at this unexpected visitor. She shooed them with her hands. Whatever Luke's father wanted to say, it wasn't for them to hear.

"Go to the kitchen and have your snack.

Shawna, you pour the milk. No arguing about it, please."

They went, jostling each other for position as they hurried through the doorway. She turned to her guest. "Sit down, please. As I said, I can't—"

"Discuss a patient. I know." He sat. This time he gave her a real smile, and she blinked, seeing Luke in another's expression. Luke the way he used to be, with the ready smile that melted the girls' hearts.

Now that she saw it, she couldn't help noticing other similarities—that strong jaw, the olive tone to the skin. Mr. Marino's hair was white, though. Distinguished looking, she supposed.

"Well, then, if you realize that—"

He spread his hands wide. "Then this is a foolish trip. I know. I just—" He shook his head. "He won't talk to me on the phone, did you know that?"

She nodded reluctantly, hating to admit she knew what should be private between father and son.

"Yes, of course you knew. You answered the phone one of the times I called." He got up and paced across the room, as if he couldn't sit still. "I know my feelings aren't your concern, but you're my only hope. Can you at least tell me how he's doing? Not medical details—just the sort of thing a layman might say."

This was shaky territory, but the plea in his voice was hard to resist. The casual observer might look at the expensive car parked in her driveway, the designer watch on his wrist, and say that here was a man who had everything. But he didn't. He didn't have a relationship with his only son.

She nodded, trying to choose her words carefully. "Well, he's stronger than you might expect after months in the hospital." She tried to think of something else positive she might say. There didn't seem to be much. "He—um, he's seen a few people." Only because she forced the issue.

"Has he? That's good. I'd heard he wasn't seeing anyone. He needs to get out and see people." Regret touched his face. "Even if he won't see me."

"I'm sorry." She was. No matter how bitter the divorce may have been, this separation between father and son had to cause pain.

His face twisted slightly. "He blames me, you see. For the divorce, for his mother's unhappiness. Maybe he's right, maybe I am to blame. But don't I deserve a chance to make it up to him?"

That wasn't a question she could answer. If people always got exactly what they deserved, Shawna and Michael wouldn't have lost their father.

Phillip Marino shook his head. "Never mind. I shouldn't put you on the spot. Just... if there's anything he needs, anything at all, let me know."

She was sorry for him, but this was yet another thing she couldn't make better, and she wasn't going to make any promises that could cause trouble with Luke. "If there's anything I think of, I'll mention it to my boss."

"Fair enough." He paused for a moment and then came toward her, holding out his hand. "Thank you, Mrs. Donnelly. It was good of you to say anything to me. And I know you're good for Luke. Just keep trying, will you?"

"I plan to." She shook hands briefly and opened the door for him, wanting him to go and take with him the hint of any impropriety in talking with a patient's father. "Good night, Mr. Marino."

For an instant he looked haggard. Then he straightened, pasted a confident look on his face and walked quickly out of her house.

* * *

At least she'd actually succeeded in getting Luke out in the car, even though he didn't seem to be enjoying it much. She glanced across at him, noting the stress in his hands, in the line of his jaw. Not good. Had she made a mistake, pushing him into this?

If so, it was too late to back out now. She was taking so much responsibility for Luke's future on her shoulders, but there didn't seem to be any other choice. At least Mr. Dickson had been enthusiastic about this expedition, willing to ensure that no one would walk in on their session.

"I thought there'd be less traffic taking the bypass this time of the evening, instead of going through town." She was babbling, she suspected, letting her response to his stress fuel hers.

"I suppose."

They approached an overpass, and Luke's hands tightened so that his knuckles were white. Something twisted inside her at the pattern. Certain things triggered a response in him—a car parked by the side of the road, an overpass. Did they remind him of danger points in the battle zone?

"The new bypass has made it a lot easier

to get to the hospital. My sister, Terry, claims the paramedic units have cut a good fifteen minutes off their runs." Babbling again. He didn't care about Terry.

But he surprised her by actually glancing her way. "Little Terry's a paramedic?"

"Little Terry's all grown up now—a fire-fighter and a paramedic. Her fiancé is head of emergency services at the hospital."

"Hard to believe." He went back to staring at the road ahead, as if only his vigilance would get them to the clinic safely.

She was doing the right thing. She had to believe that. The longer Luke hid inside that house, the harder it would be to get out. Her thoughts flickered to Frank, and his stories about coming back from World War II. Had his wife had to use tough love to keep him going when his mind was playing tricks on him?

Not that it was love, tough or otherwise, that she felt for Luke. Just the affection she'd have for any old friend and the natural concern for a fellow creature who was hurting. That was all.

She flicked on the turn signal and headed for the exit ramp. "Almost there." Her voice sounded as artificially cheerful as it had when she'd driven Kenny to the hospital for the chemo treatments.

She pulled into the clinic parking lot. The long, low building seemed to crouch next to the massive bulk of Providence Hospital behind it. She passed the lighted main entrance and pulled up at the side door nearest the therapy pool.

"Here we are." Sliding out, she glanced at her watch. They were right on time, and this wing of the building should be deserted. After opening the trunk, she pulled the wheelchair out.

This had better work. *Please, Lord, let it work.*

She took a deep breath and pushed the chair toward the passenger door. Luke was ready, and he managed the transfer from car to chair with relative ease. Working with weights was increasing the upper-body strength he needed if he were to begin getting out of that chair.

She closed and locked the car, then turned back to find Luke frowning at her.

"You'd better be right about this, Mary Kate. If I go in there and find one person gawking at me—"

"You won't," she said crisply. Even if he

did, this was the one place where no one would gawk. Everyone here either had troubles of their own or had seen it all before. Still, she didn't think she'd tell him that.

She pushed the chair up the ramp, breathing a silent prayer.

Fifteen minutes later, she'd moved from terrified that she was pushing him too hard to cautiously optimistic. Luke had handled getting into the building and changing clothes with more ease than she'd expected— and probably than he had expected, too. Surely he wouldn't back out now that he could see the tempting azure water.

"You really are getting stronger, you know. And the water will help your flexibility and balance."

She maneuvered the chair across the tile floor toward the small therapeutic pool. Her hair was already kinking into curls from the moisture, and the aroma of chlorine reminded her of the children's swim classes at the Y. And, further back, high school swim team. Luke had excelled at that, as he had at anything athletic.

Luke stopped the chair at the head of the ramp. "Will it make me the way I was?" Bitterness threaded his voice.

It hurt her, but she wouldn't show that.

"Was I sounding like Pollyanna again? Sorry." She picked up a flotation belt and held it out to him.

He shook his head. "I can swim."

"I remember. But the rules are strict." She smiled. "Besides, I can grab you by it if you start to swim away."

He grunted his disapproval, but fastened the belt over the T-shirt he wore with cutoff sweatpants. She wore a T-shirt, too, over her tank suit. She wouldn't have thought twice about pulling it off with one of her elderly stroke patients, but she couldn't help feeling more reticent with Luke.

When he was ready, she grabbed the chair handles. "We'll take the chair right down the ramp into the water. Some of my stroke patients find this scary, but I guess you can take it."

"I can take it. That doesn't mean I like it."

"You really have to stop being so pleasant and cooperative," she teased. "I might get the idea you're enjoying this."

"I didn't mean—"

The words cut off abruptly when he hit the warm water. Almost before she'd stopped the chair, he launched himself from it, reaching the opposite side of the pool in a few strong strokes, and giving her no opportunity to grab the belt and stop him.

"Hey, no fair. How am I supposed to catch you when you're that fast?" She shoved the wheelchair into place and turned back to him.

He submerged, swimming underwater and surfacing next to her with a splash that drenched her T-shirt. He grabbed the bar and righted himself, water streaming from his dark hair. His face—her breath caught.

This wasn't the withdrawn, bitter face she'd almost become used to. This was Luke the way he used to be—strong, laughing, in his element. It wrenched her heart with its reminder of things past. She struggled to regain control, to be again the competent professional who thought only of him as a patient, not a man.

He caught her wrist in a wet, warm grip. "I know I fought you every step of the way. You were right. This—" his nod took in the pool "—this is worth getting out of the house for."

She would not let him see that his words touched her. And she certainly wouldn't let him guess at the waves of attraction that went through her at his touch. But she couldn't kid herself about its power.

"Good." Her voice sounded a bit shaky, and she cleared her throat. "But we didn't just come here to play. Hold the bar and put your feet down. It's time to get some work done."

Chapter Six

He'd slept better last night than he had in months, without a single disturbing dream to wake him up. The effect of exercising in the pool, probably. Luke had to admit that Mary Kate had been right about that, although confessing that to her wouldn't be a good idea. She was already too convinced that she knew what was best for him.

Didn't she? If he were being honest with himself, he'd face the fact that her predictions were, in some cases, coming true. He still didn't have much confidence that he'd ever get out of the chair, but he'd begun to feel as if he'd at least be able to take care of himself. Nobody else, of course, but himself. That was enough.

He glanced toward the door at the sound

of footsteps. Mary Kate was a few minutes late, unheard-of for her. The minute he saw her face, he realized that something was up. Her gaze refused to meet his.

"I'm so sorry, but I—" A faint color came up in her cheeks.

"Out with it, M.K. What's wrong?" Maybe she felt, as he did, that their relationship had changed somehow with that trip to the pool, becoming less therapist/patient and more... more what? He didn't know the answer to that.

She gestured toward the door behind her. "It's a teacher in-service day today, so the kids are off school. And my sitter arrangements fell through. I know it's an imposition, but would you mind if the children played quietly in the kitchen while we work? I guess I should have called, but—"

"But you figured that if you gave me advance notice, I'd try to cancel the session," he finished for her. He shrugged, vaguely surprised that he didn't seem to mind so much having his home invaded by her kids. "It's okay. Certainly not worth getting upset about."

Something startled and wary came into her eyes, as if he'd said something alarming.

Then it was gone, so quickly he might have imagined it.

"Thank you. It's just that it's so unprofessional to show up for your therapy with my kids in tow."

She opened the door, letting Shawna and Michael in. Michael ran straight to him, as if they were old friends. Shawna hung back a little, but he didn't think it was because the wheelchair put her off. Maybe she was just enough older than her brother to have shed some of that unconscious openness.

"Mommy said you went to the pool." Michael leaned against the chair, his blue eyes wide. "Did you like going swimming again?"

For an instant he was cutting through the water, feeling the strength in his arms, the flow of water like silk against his skin. "Yes, I sure did. Do you and Shawna know how to swim?"

"We're taking lessons at the Y." Shawna answered for both of them. "If we get good enough, we can be on the swim team." She tugged Michael's arm. "Come on. You know what Mom said. We have to take our stuff into the kitchen and stay out of the way."

He watched them go, with Shawna shepherding her little brother along. Then he wheeled the chair into the dining room, where Mary Kate was fussing with the equipment. "Shawna's quite the little mother, isn't she?"

Her eyes widened just as Michael's did. "Do you think so? I always just seem to hear them scrapping. Or rolling around on the floor like a couple of puppies, although Shawna's less likely to do that anymore. She's getting too grown-up, I suppose. Or thinks she is."

"They probably save their fighting for you."

She smiled, but he thought there was something worried behind the expression. It couldn't be easy, even with the support of her family, to be both mother and father to those kids.

Well, it wasn't his business. He had enough to deal with, without worrying about Mary Kate's family life.

"What torture do you have in mind for me today?"

She patted the parallel bars that Gabe and Seth had set up. "I think you're ready to put some weight on your legs."

"No." That couldn't be fear he felt, could it? "I'm not ready."

"I think you are. Come on, just give it a try."

"And break something when I fall? No, thanks."

It was unreasonable of her to ask it. Or maybe unreasonable of him to refuse—he wasn't sure which, and he didn't like not being sure.

She pushed at the mats she'd shoved under and around the bars. "Falling is part of it. Remember when you learned to ice-skate? But you have nice soft mats to fall on instead of ice."

He gritted his teeth. "You're talking to me like I'm about six again."

"I refuse to say the obvious answer to that—it wouldn't be professional."

"In other words, stop acting like I'm six." He wanted to lash out at her with anger, but it was becoming harder and harder to do that.

She bent toward him, putting her hands over his. "Come on, Luke. You can't kid me. I saw how strong you were in the pool. You can take your weight on your arms as much as you want. Just give it a try, like you did the pool. That worked out, didn't it?"

"I suppose." She was right. He did sound like a sulky kid. He may as well admit it. "All right, I confess. The pool was a good idea, even if getting there—"

He stopped. Some things Mary Kate didn't need to know, like the unpleasant aftermath of being in battle.

She moved the chair into position, seeming to take his acceptance for granted. "I guess it's hard, getting out again. Hard not to keep your guard up all the time, the way you had to over there."

She saw more than he'd thought. He grunted in response, and then pushed the words out. "Overpasses. Vehicles parked along the road. Something that looks like a breakdown. Any of those could be an ambush, or a bomb planted to go off just when you go by."

"I've heard about the roadside bombings on the news, but I guess I didn't realize what it would be like. Didn't they give you any help in dealing with that when you were in the military hospital?"

"Required sessions with a shrink that are supposed to do the trick." He shrugged. "I couldn't see that it did, but maybe I'd be in worse shape without them." Amazing, that he could say to her what he hadn't verbalized to anyone else.

She helped him get a grip on the bars and then braced her feet, preparing to help him up. "It'll take some time to get over."

If she'd oozed sympathy, he wouldn't have been able to take it, but her calm, matter-of-fact tone made it possible to verbalize the thoughts that lurked at the back of his mind. "What if I don't?"

"You will." She sounded serenely confident. "Just like you're going to conquer these bars. Ready?"

She had a firm grip on him. He wanted to say she wasn't strong enough, but he'd worked with her long enough to know that wasn't true. She was strong—with him, and with her kids. Probably spiritually, too, in order to cope with Kenny's loss and still hold on to the serenity of hers.

"Ready." He tightened his grip, trying to imagine he was plunging off the high dive for the first time, and muscled himself to an upright position. For an instant it was dizzying, and then quite suddenly he was exhilarated. He was standing for the first time in months.

"All right—great. Don't try to move. Just let yourself get used to the feeling. Then slowly let your legs take some of the weight."

"I'm okay." He wasn't, not really. His arm muscles trembled from the effort of keeping his body vertical and he could feel sweat break out on his forehead. He tried to focus on one of the stylized flowers in the wall-paper.

"That's enough for the first time. Let me ease you down again."

"No." He bit off the word. "I'm going to take a step."

Mary Kate's arm tightened around him. "Not yet."

He didn't bother to answer, frowning, concentrating, trying to drag his right leg forward by sheer force of will. Finally it moved, inching ahead.

"Terrific! Come on, now, let's not overdo the first time—"

He was already forcing his left leg forward. It was moving, but his arm muscles trembled, he was losing his grip, he—

The mat rushed toward him, but Mary Kate's arms were around him, breaking his fall as she went down with him.

"Are you all right?" Concern flooded her voice as she grabbed his shoulder. "Luke, talk to me."

"I'm fine." He opened his eyes. Mary Kate's face was inches away, so close he could almost touch that soft skin. "You told me I'd fall, didn't you?"

Her breath came out in a rush of relief.

"I didn't really mean it. Are you sure nothing hurts?"

"Only my pride." He ought to feel angry that she'd pushed him into this, or disappointed that he hadn't been able to do more. Instead he felt good, better than he had in months.

Maybe that was because he'd made progress. Or maybe it was because his arms were around Mary Kate, and she was looking at him with caring, affection—

His breath quickened. She wasn't looking at him the way a therapist looked at a patient. No, it was more the way a woman looked at a man she cared for—lips parted slightly, eyes darkening, skin flushing.

For an instant he leaned toward her. Another inch and their lips would touch—

He pulled back abruptly, breathing as if he'd been running. This couldn't happen. It was about the worst mistake he could possibly make, and just because Mary Kate was warm and sweet and cared about him was no reason to act like a fool.

She blinked, color rising in her cheeks, and turned away. "Maybe—maybe I'd better get some lunch ready." Her voice sounded husky.

"Good idea." He forced the words out. "We need a break."

From the work, and also from each other.

Mary Kate spread peanut butter on a slice of bread so fiercely that the bread tore. She bit her lip and forced herself to be calm. Thank goodness Luke was leaving her alone in the kitchen. She needed breathing space to cope with what had happened between them.

This wasn't just her, feeling a reminiscent attraction for an old high school crush. Both of them had felt it, she knew by the way Luke had looked at her, as if he'd been ready to kiss her. As if, in another instant, their lips would have met.

And he'd been the one to turn away first. Her cheeks flamed and she blinked back hot tears. How could she have done that? It was wrong on so many levels. She was Luke's therapist, and that was the only relationship they could have.

To say nothing of the guilt that swept over her at the thought of Kenny. Feeling something for Luke or any other man was being disloyal to him.

She slapped the slices of bread together and cut them into triangles. All right, Mary

Kate, get a grip. It's not the worst thing that's happened in your life.

She didn't run and hide at the first sign of trouble. She held her chin up and she coped. So she and Luke were attracted to each other. All right. That didn't mean they were going to act on that attraction.

She certainly wasn't. She'd been caught off guard, but it wouldn't happen again. Even if Luke hadn't been her patient, she had her hands full with kids, family, job, adjusting to life without Kenny. There was no space left for romance.

And Luke's reaction certainly showed that he didn't want anything, either. So she'd put a smile on her face and act as if nothing had happened.

She arranged sandwiches on plates, poured milk and then went looking for the kids. Shawna was on the back porch, absorbed in a game of jacks. But Michael—

Then she heard voices, coming from the workshop behind the kitchen. Michael was in the shop with Luke.

Fine. She had to face Luke, in any event. It may as well be now.

She took a step toward the workshop door, forcing a smile onto stiff lips. Another step, and she could hear Michael's voice. She froze, unable to move.

"See, my daddy started making the car with me, but we didn't get to finish it." His childish treble might have shaken a bit on the words. "I thought maybe you could help me finish it, 'cause you have this neat workshop and all."

Pain twisted her heart. She hadn't seen that unfinished car in months and hadn't dreamed that Michael still had it. What else was he hiding behind that brave little facade?

She pushed herself to take the few steps into the workshop. "Hey, is anyone ready for lunch?"

"Mary Kate—" Luke began, his face troubled.

She silenced him with a fierce glare. This wasn't any of his business. She'd deal with it in her own way.

"I have sandwiches ready for you and Shawna. You can take them out onto the back porch and have a picnic."

She shooed Michael through the kitchen and onto the porch, taking her time settling the two of them with their milk and sandwiches. Hoping that by the time she went back inside, Luke would have sense enough to avoid the subject.

She could see at a glance that that hope was futile. Luke's dark brows were drawn together in a frown, and he had both hands planted on the arms of the chair as if he'd like to propel himself out of it. She closed the door carefully behind her.

"I don't want to talk about it." She went quickly across to the counter, where she had a plate ready for him, and transferred it to the table. "Would you like water or iced tea with your sandwiches?"

"What I'd like is for you to stop fussing about food and discuss this."

Her temper flared. She spun toward him, planting her fists on her hips. "It's between me and Michael. It's none of your business."

"Michael made it my business when he brought the subject up. You don't think I suggested working on anything with him, do you?"

"No." Anger made her say more than she should. "I think you're too busy thinking about yourself."

She swung away from him, appalled at her unbridled tongue. Before she could come up with an apology, he'd wheeled over next to her and jerked a chair out from the kitchen table.

"Sit," he growled. "I'm not having an argument with you when I have to crane my neck."

That was another mistake she tried not to make, and something else she needed to apologize for. She knew better than to force a person in a wheelchair to keep looking up at her.

The trouble was, she didn't have the least desire to apologize. She sank down on the chair, sure she looked like Shawna having a case of the sulks.

Forgive me, Lord. I'm behaving badly, I know. I just don't want anyone coming that far into my children's confidence, and especially not Luke.

"Sorry." She managed to look at him. "It's just that the car is a sensitive subject for me."

"Probably for Michael, too." His voice went softer, the anger in it easing. "First off, the good Lord knows I'm not ready to take on responsibility for anybody or anything. If that makes me selfish, well, I figure that's my right."

She swallowed, trying to ease the tightness in her throat. "I am sorry. I shouldn't have said that. But Michael—"

"Tell me." He grabbed her hands when she

would have turned away, holding them firmly between his. "What does that car mean?"

She took a deep breath and let it out. She couldn't get out of telling him now.

"Kenny had made one with Shawna, when her class did the project. Michael loved it and just couldn't wait until he went to school to make one, so Kenny started one with him." Her voice softened as she remembered the two of them, heads together over the kitchen table, making a mess just when she was trying to get supper on.

"Michael couldn't have been old enough to do much of it." Luke's fingers moved gently against her hands. Comforting.

"No, he wasn't. But Kenny had such patience with the kids. Far more than I do, I'm afraid. He'd let Michael work on it, no matter how long it took. But then—" Her throat closed.

"That's when Kenny got sick." He seemed to understand what she couldn't say.

She nodded. "It was such a shock, and it went so fast. You think you have all the time in the world, and suddenly you don't have any."

"I'm sorry."

She couldn't accuse him of not caring

about anyone else now. His voice was warm with concern and caring.

"Thank you." She cleared her throat. "The car just seemed to disappear, and with everything that was going on, I didn't even notice. Obviously Michael kept it, and now he wants to finish it for the class project."

She'd offered to help him make something for the project, and he'd said no. And now her son had gone to someone who was a virtual stranger for help with his precious car.

"What do you want me to do?"

She shook her head, longing to find some way of dealing with this that didn't involve Luke. "You could tell him you can't."

"I'm not going to lie to the boy." Luke leaned toward her, his hands still holding hers, his dark gaze very intent. "I didn't ask for this, and I certainly won't do anything without your permission. But Michael came to me, and I won't turn him down. If you want to do that, it's up to you."

"Easy. Don't try to move it so far at one time." Mary Kate kept a steadying hand on Luke's back as he leaned on the metal walker.

"Baby steps," he grunted.

"That's right, baby steps. There's nothing wrong with taking it one small step at a time."

At the moment, the only step she felt capable of taking was to concentrate on this therapy session and ignore everything that had happened in the week and a half since Luke first attempted the bars. She would not start obsessing about Michael's request or Luke's surprising reaction.

She still struggled with what to do about that. She couldn't put Michael off much longer.

And, to be honest, she could hardly blame Luke. If he was willing to help Michael, who seemed able to get through some chink in his armor, why should he look like the bad guy over something that was her decision?

She'd felt a wave of thankfulness when Michael had accepted her statement that she had to think about whether Luke could help him with the car. After all, Luke was still recuperating, even if he was moving with astonishing speed now that he'd actually gotten his legs under him.

His upper-body strength was certainly increasing. He must be working out with the weights even when she wasn't here. She could feel it in the hard muscles under her hand as he forced the walker forward a few inches, into a patch of afternoon sunlight that streaked across the narrow wooden floorboards. The light glittered on shiny metal, emphasizing the walker. No one who hadn't been in this spot could possibly imagine how much sheer will and work it was taking Luke to move.

"Good job." She had to keep encouraging, even if he accused her again of talking to him as if he were a child. Everyone needed encouragement. "Think you can make it to the edge of the archway?"

Another three feet, but it undoubtedly looked like three miles to Luke. Still, he wasn't giving up and he wasn't complaining, and that in itself was progress. Just being up on his feet, even for a short period each day, couldn't help but improve his outlook.

He edged forward again, perspiration beading on his forehead. "You think I can't do it, don't you?"

That little flicker of competitiveness encouraged her. If she could just help him see this as a challenge, it would make a huge difference. "I'd say it's a good test of how tough you are."

His muscles tightened again, his T-shirt damp under her touch, and she caught him as he struggled for balance. He righted himself slowly, pulling away from her hands. "Let me do it by myself."

That was farther than she'd intended him to go. She'd have to find just the right incentive to push him along at an appropriate pace. She took her hand off him but hovered on the alert, ready to grab him if necessary.

Sweating, straining as if he were running a marathon, he forced his legs to work. She held her breath, her whole body straining toward him, willing him to succeed. All her earlier irritation with him had been swallowed up by his struggle.

You can do it. You can. Just try. She bit her lip, forcing herself not to touch him as he fought both with the walker and with his own body.

"Just one more step, and you'll be there." She measured the line from the edge of the archway with her eye, waiting for him to cross the imaginary finish line. Once he'd burst the tape with his classmates cheering—now he battled toward a crack in the floor.

One final surge, and he made it. She caught him by the waist. "That's terrific, Luke. Really great. Just stand still while I bring the chair over."

She turned away to get the wheelchair, but even as she grabbed it, she saw that he was still moving. "Wait a minute." She shoved the chair next to him. "That's plenty for today."

"No." He ground out the word. "I can make it to the carpet."

Short of knocking him over, she couldn't stop him. She slid the chair alongside him, heart in her throat, as he stubbornly covered another couple of feet to the edge of the rug before sliding into the chair.

She had to swallow the tears that choked her throat before she could speak. "I suppose there's no point in lecturing you about listening to me. But that was fantastic. I'd never dreamed you could go that far your first day with the walker."

Luke leaned back in the chair, eyes closed, sweat glistening on his olive skin. He shrugged, a restless movement of his shoulders. "Doesn't mean anything."

"Not mean anything?" She resisted the urge to shake him. "It means you're on your feet again. It means you'll soon be getting around without the chair. Don't you see how good this is?"

"Can you make me the way I was?" He opened his eyes to glare at her. "Can you?"

Her heart lurched. He already knew the answer, but if he wanted to hear her say it, she'd be honest with him. She slid onto the nearest chair, bringing herself to his level. "No. I can't. Nobody can do that. But that doesn't mean you can't live a normal life."

"If I can't be the way I was, then I can't be a cop."

That was the first time he'd spoken of the job he'd left when his unit was called up. She should have realized it was eating at him.

"They'll find something for you, won't they?" She wasn't sure what obligation the police force had, but surely they wouldn't just cut him loose because he'd been injured fighting for his country.

"A desk job." Bitterness laced his voice. "That's what they'll offer me."

"Isn't that important, too?" She was probably sounding like Pollyanna again. "Gabe has found a lot of satisfaction in teaching since he can't be on the fire line."

He shrugged, turning away slightly, no doubt trying to keep her from seeing how much it mattered to him. "I guess I'm not like Gabe. For me, it's a pretty poor substitute for the rush of being on the street."

The rush. She might have known. "Is that

all you men think about? You're addicted to that adrenaline rush, just like my brothers and Kenny, charging into dangerous situations as much for the thrill as because it's the job."

His eyes snapped back to hers. "Kenny didn't die because of that."

Her breath caught, and she jerked back as if he'd hit her. Before she could find words, he caught her hands.

"I'm sorry. That was stupid. Really stupid. I didn't mean it." He leaned toward her, guilt filling his face.

"It doesn't matter." She tried to pull her hands free, but he didn't let go.

"Look, maybe you have a point. Maybe it is the rush, but that can be a good thing. Anybody who's been there can tell you that it's only the adrenaline that keeps you going. It probably kept me alive. It's kind of hard to come down from that."

"Okay, I get that." Now it was her turn to clasp his hands in her urgent need to make him understand. "But can't you put that same thing to use in making a recovery?"

His face tightened, the skin straining over the strong bone structure. "It's different."

"How?" She wasn't going to let him off

the hook if she had a clue as to what would help him.

For a long moment he didn't speak, and when he did, his lips were so tense it was a wonder he could get the words out. "Before—well, I could use that adrenaline to keep my people and myself alive. I was strong enough to deal with whatever they threw at us." His face twisted. "I let everyone down when I got hurt. Now I don't have anything left to give."

The shadows in his eyes told her that there was more to it than he was telling her. Maybe, someday, he would tell her the rest.

To protect and to serve—that was the motto he'd lived his life by and now, even if he didn't realize it, he needed to experience that feeling again, even in the smallest of ways.

And she had the power to make that happen, if she could get past her own hurt and reluctance.

"I hope you have something left to give." She held his hands between hers, not letting him turn away. "Because you said you'd help my son, and we're not going to let you back down on that."

Chapter Seven

"Are you sure you both have everything you need for school today?" Mary Kate glanced in the rearview mirror. Shawna and Michael both looked a little droopy this morning. No one had slept well the previous night. Michael had wakened twice with bad dreams, and Shawna seemed to be coming down with a cold, which probably meant all three of them would catch it.

"Yes, Mommy," they chorused, managing to sound bored in unison.

Two more blocks to the school, and she hadn't yet found the words to talk to Michael about the model car. Still, sometimes the best heart-to-hearts took place in the car. For an instant she felt light-headed. There were too many cars in her thoughts right now—the one in which she spent so much time, the model that meant something to Michael he hadn't yet verbalized, the car that sat in Luke's garage, ignored and abandoned.

She realized she was gripping the steering wheel too tightly and forced her fingers to relax. Relax—that was good advice. Remember those long conversations with Mom, driving home from cheerleading or a movie, the darkness outside seeming to create a private cocoon in which she could say almost anything.

"Michael, I talked to Mr. Marino yesterday about the model car."

In the rearview mirror, she could see the wary expression on his small face. "He said we should call him Luke."

"Luke, then." She wasn't going to get sidetracked into the proper way to address an adult. "He said he'd help you with it, if it's okay with me."

His eyes lit up. "Is it, Mommy? I won't pester him, I promise."

"I know, honey." She hesitated, framing what she wanted to say, not wanting it to sound accusing. "I didn't know you still had the car. I hadn't seen it in a long time." She'd found it hard to believe when he'd produced the car from a shoe box in the back of his closet.

He shrugged, frowning down at his shoes, apparently feeling that didn't need an answer. She'd have to be more direct.

"Why didn't you tell me that you wanted to finish the car when we were talking about the class project?"

Again he shrugged. "I don't know."

"Was it because you thought I wouldn't help you with it?"

His smile broke through. "You don't know how to make a car model, Mommy."

There was a lot she hadn't known how to do before Kenny's illness. She'd had to learn in a hurry.

"Well, that's true, but maybe I could have found someone to help. I just want to know why you didn't tell me about it."

He studied his shoes some more. "I didn't want to make you sad."

The words robbed her of speech. For an instant all she could do was try to control the hurt. Her little boy had tried to protect her at the cost of his own pain. Why hadn't she seen what was happening?

She stared out the windshield, focusing on the School Zone sign, and pushed her emotions back into hiding. She cleared her throat. "That was very thoughtful of you. But I'd rather be sad and know what's going on with you. That's what moms do. Okay?"

"Okay, Mommy. When do I get to work on the car?" He was single-minded, as always.

"Today after school. I brought it with me. Grammy will pick you up and bring you to Luke's house." She considered adding her usual cautions to behave properly, but maybe she'd done that enough.

Besides, they were pulling into the school driveway already. "Shawna, if you want to go to Casey Duncan's house instead, that's all right."

"No." Shawna turned away, picking up her backpack. "That's okay. I think maybe she's busy today."

Something about that averted face put Mary Kate on alert. "Is something wrong? Did you and Casey have a fight?" The two girls had been best friends since kindergarten, and their spats were rare but fierce when they happened.

"Nothing's wrong." Shawna's tone was almost curt enough to be rude. Almost, but not quite.

"Shawnie—" But they had already drawn

up to the drop-off point, and she couldn't delay without having the cars behind her start beeping.

"See you later, Mom." Shawna slid out quickly, turning away without even a wave.

"Bye, Mommy." Michael had decided recently that a first-grader shouldn't kiss his mother in front of his friends, but he leaned between the seats for a hug.

"Have a good day." She watched him start toward the building, absorbed in an instant by a clutch of first-grade boys.

A beep from behind recalled her, and she put the car in gear and pulled out. She could see the front of the school in her rearview mirror. It showed her Michael's crew, racing into the building, jostling each other.

It also showed her Shawna, walking up the three steps to the doors. Mary Kate frowned. Surely that was Casey, sitting on the low brick wall with a couple of other girls. They were chattering together almost ostentatiously, and no one made any gesture toward Shawna.

Shawna went past, eyes straight ahead. Her head was held high with confidence, but something about the small, straight figure with the red curls tumbling onto her jean jacket looked lonely, almost forlorn.

The car behind her beeped again, and Mary Kate pulled out onto the street, frowning, her mother's intuition going into overdrive. Something was wrong, and Shawna wasn't telling her. Did she, like Michael, have the mistaken idea that she had to protect her mother from knowing the truth?

"There you go." Mary Kate set a brimming bowl of homemade vegetable soup, rich with beef and tomatoes, in front of Luke on the kitchen table. Its aroma tickled her nostrils, making her realize she hadn't taken much time for breakfast that morning. "You won't find better soup than that no matter where you go."

"Complimenting yourself?" He raised a jet-black eyebrow as he picked up the spoon.

"No, complimenting my mother." She ladled soup into a bowl for herself and slid onto the chair opposite him. "She makes a huge pot of soup about once a week, and the rest of us are the beneficiaries. When the boys were single, that was probably the only decent meal they had all week, except for Sunday dinner, of course."

He took a spoonful, then another. His taut features seemed to relax as the warmth and flavor hit him. "For soup like this, it might be worth going hungry the rest of the time. Give your mother my compliments."

"If I do, she'll probably show up at your door with a quart or two. You won't chase her away, will you?"

For an instant she thought he'd take offense at this reminder of his attitude toward the people from church who'd tried to bring him meals. Then he smiled slightly. "No, I guess not."

She felt tension ease, too. They'd fallen into the habit of having lunch together on days when they did a double session. It saved her from running home to have lunch, she'd told him, and that was true enough. But it was also a way to make sure he had a decent meal once in a while.

She never could resist the urge to feed people, but she'd come by it honestly. Her mother had set the example when she was too young to realize that everyone didn't send a hot meal to the elderly widower down the block or a batch of homemade cookies to the harried young single mom across the street. It hadn't occurred to Mary Kate until she was grown that sharing food was both a way of expressing love and a ministry for her mother.

Luke looked better these days, either

because he was eating more or because of the therapy. Or both. The color was back in his cheeks and his eyes had begun to regain their old sparkle. Unfortunately, even though she was happy to see it, the reminder of the old Luke just seemed to make the attraction she felt more insistent.

He glanced up, catching her studying his face, and she looked away. She crumbled a cracker into the soup, even though she didn't like it that way, and tried to think of something nice and neutral to say.

"After you've had a break, maybe we ought to try going outside with the walker. Getting around there is a bit harder than walking across an even floor."

Lines formed between his brows. "Just in the backyard."

Where no one would see him. She could finish that thought for him with no trouble. "That's a good place to start." *But sooner or later I'm going to get you out in public, and that will be a giant step forward. You'll see.*

He sipped more soup and then paused, spoon balanced in his long fingers. "Are you sure you can stay for another session this afternoon? I thought originally the army approved one session a day."

The question came out of the blue, reminding her forcefully of the visit from his father. Of the fact that his father was paying for all this extra time she was spending.

"The director decided you'd benefit from more sessions. There are extra disability benefits, you know." That was true enough, but she hated skirting around the issue, feeling as if she kept something from him.

His dark gaze leveled on her face, as if probing for subterfuge. "You're not doing this on your own time, are you? I don't need charity."

Relief at the form his suspicion took made her almost light-headed. "No, I promise I'm being paid. I'm only part-time at the clinic, and I'm actually doing better than I expected to this month, thanks to you."

He nodded, but she thought some trace of suspicion lingered in his eyes. Or maybe that was only the guilt she felt at her inability to tell him everything.

Still, the rules were clear. She wasn't free to divulge anything about the arrangements Luke's father had made with the clinic. And if she had been, how would Luke react? She probably knew the answer to that one without even thinking. Given his aversion to charity and the fact that he wouldn't so much as speak with his father on the phone, Luke would reject that help in an instant, and the progress he'd been making could easily come to a halt.

But that didn't make her stop feeling guilty. Kenny had always said she didn't have a face designed for hiding anything. She got up abruptly.

"I think I heard the letter carrier. I'll bring the mail in." She probably should expect Luke to do that himself, but the urge to escape for a moment was too overwhelming.

By the time she returned to the kitchen with a sheaf of mail in her hand, she was confident that she'd managed to steer away from the touchy subject. "Looks as if you got quite a haul today." She plopped the mail down in front of him on the kitchen table and began clearing the dishes.

Paper rustled as he sorted through them. "Bill, bill, advertisement, coupon to have my tires rotated, a newsletter from the church."

"Sounds like my mail, except that there are usually a few more bills." She spoke lightly, but there was more truth to that than she'd let on to anyone. She'd always taken care of the finances, even when Kenny was alive, but then she hadn't had to worry about having enough in the account to cover the bills.

Luke was ripping open an envelope when she turned back to the table. He scanned the sheet, then seemed to freeze for an instant. He tossed it onto the table. "I suppose you got one of those, too."

Curious, she leaned over to look at it. "Our high school reunion—no, but maybe it will come today for me, too. Has it really been that long?" She sat down on the chair next to him, picking up the letter to glance through it.

"Seems longer." His hand had tightened into a fist, the muscles standing out on his forearm, propped on the table. "Somehow I don't think I'll attend."

She wanted to put her hand over his, to soothe away the stress. She didn't. "It's not until August. Maybe you'll have changed your mind by then."

"Will you go?"

The question caught her on the raw. Go to the reunion without Kenny? Not likely. "I guess not."

He took the letter from her, tossing it in the direction of the wastebasket. "We're in the same boat. Neither of us feels up to facing our old classmates now."

"Well, not en masse, anyway. I've stayed good friends with a few of them. Marcy Allwood and Karen Tripler, especially."

"I remember. The three of you were always together. Made it tough for a guy to get any one of you alone."

She lifted her eyebrows. "Really? I never noticed you having any trouble. As I recall, you dated all three of us. Separately, of course."

"You're making that up. I never went out with Karen, and I only took Marcy to a movie once because her cousin kept trying to fix us up."

She shook her head, smiling a little at how naive they'd all been. "Fix us up. Now there's an expression I haven't heard in a while. Thank goodness. Now that I stop and think about it, half the class was usually trying to fix up the other half with someone."

"I didn't need any pushing to ask you out. Just an extra measure of guts, given how protective your brothers and cousin were."

"I'm sure they scared you to death," she teased. "You're just lucky they didn't come after you when we broke up." She could say the words lightly. It was a long time ago. Puppy love.

"I was kind of surprised about that. You must not have told them what happened."

She shrugged, the memory coming back too clearly for comfort. "You went out with Sally Friedman when you were supposed to be going steady with me."

When you'd held me close the night before and told me that you loved me. When you'd convinced me there was no one else in the world for you. Maybe it had been puppy love, but it had hurt like crazy all the same.

"Yeah." He looked down at his hands, as if he didn't want to look at her. As if, after all these years, the memory embarrassed him. "I was stupid."

She wouldn't let him see that she cared. "Why? After all, most of the varsity football team wanted to go out with Sally. I don't blame you for picking her over me."

"I said I was stupid, not that I was a total idiot." He looked at her then, and the emotion in his dark eyes startled her. "I wasn't picking Sally over you. I was running scared."

She stared at him blankly. "Scared? Of what?"

"Of myself." He touched the back of her hand, a gentle, featherlight stroke. "I was head over heels for you. I'd never felt that way about anyone, and it scared the life out of me. So I did the first thing I thought of to put some distance between us."

She couldn't speak for a moment. She shouldn't be feeling so ridiculously pleased over the idea that he'd broken up with her because he'd cared too much. She certainly couldn't let him know what she felt, but she was afraid he saw too much.

"I'm sure Sally will be at the reunion," she said lightly.

His fingers tightened over hers. "That's another good reason not to go. I'd need you to protect me."

She smiled, as she was sure he'd intended. But her pulse was beating way too fast, and all this talk of old times had made it more difficult to keep things on an even keel between them.

And that was what they both wanted, wasn't it?

He kept making the same mistake over and over. He'd told himself anything other than a patient/therapist relationship with Mary Kate was out of the question. He'd vowed to keep things cool and professional. And yet there he'd been again, talking about old times and re-membering feelings he'd put away years ago.

"This way." Luke put his hand over Michael's small one, showing him how to shape the wooden block they were turning into a car. And now he was getting involved with her kids, of all things. Was he asking for grief? He could barely be responsible for himself. He certainly couldn't for anyone else, especially a kid.

"I see." Michael's face was intent, absurdly like Mary Kate's expression when she worked on something new with him. "Daddy showed me, but I guess I forgot." His face clouded suddenly, and Luke realized he knew why.

"It'll come back to you." He kept his voice light. "Sometimes we think we forget something or someone, but it's all stored away up here." He tapped Michael's red curls. "Or maybe in here." He touched his chest.

"Mommy says Daddy is always alive in our hearts." His forehead wrinkled, as if that didn't quite satisfy him. "I want to finish the car for him."

"I see." It was tough to speak normally over the lump in his throat. "Well, then, we'd better do a really good job."

Michael frowned at the fender he was trying to round. "Could you do this part? My fingers are getting in the way."

He hesitated, but the boy was right in sensing that he didn't have the necessary dexterity yet for some of the finer points. "Sure thing."

He took the car, a little surprised by how his hands seemed to remember of their own how to use the tools. He reached up to turn on the light above the workbench. "There, now we can see better."

"You're pretty good at that." Michael leaned confidingly against his chair. "Did your daddy teach you?"

"Yes, he did." It wasn't the boy's fault that he touched a sore spot with those words. "I haven't done this in a long time, though. I might be a little rusty."

"It's a neat workshop. If I had one, I bet I could build almost anything. I could even build a birdhouse for Mommy."

"Does your mother want a birdhouse?"

He nodded. "To hang in the tree by the porch. Like Grammy has by her back porch, and the little wrens live in it and they're not scared of you at all unless you get really noisy."

"I guess noise would scare them." He held out the car for inspection. "How does that look?"

"That's a good job. Will you do the other fenders, please?"

"Yep." Funny how a skill came back to a person after all this time. He'd stopped woodworking because it reminded him of his father, but there was pleasure just in the doing.

"You know, I hid the car from Mommy."

Michael had apparently decided he was someone to confide in. It startled Luke. He'd think, with all those uncles, the boy would have picked someone else. Still, if Michael wanted to talk, he couldn't very well push him away.

"Why did you do that?" He kept his focus on the car, letting the boy talk as he wanted, without pressure.

"I thought it would make Mommy sad. Lots of things made her sad after Daddy went to Heaven."

They'd stumbled into theological territory too quickly. He wasn't a good person to talk about God's designs, not with his own doubts and questions.

"I can understand that. She probably needed to cry a lot."

Michael shook his head decidedly. "She didn't cry—not where me and Shawnie could see. But sometimes her eyes got all funny, and we knew she was feeling sad."

That was Mary Kate, all right. Trying to

keep a stiff upper lip and take care of everyone else while hiding her own pain.

He'd been doing what he thought was a decent job of that until he'd come home. Until he'd seen her again, to be exact. Then he'd unloaded all his anger and bitterness on her. Not a very pretty picture, was it?

"Well, your mother knows about the car now, so that's good."

"She said that she'd rather know about stuff, even if it makes her sad. She says that's what mommies do."

"They sure do." He ruffled Michael's red curls. "I'd say your mommy is pretty good at that, too."

And however much it cost her, she'd never let her children see. It had to be tearing her up inside, and nobody could help her with that one.

Funny. He was actually thinking about somebody else's problems for a change, instead of his own.

"Michael." Shawna called from the kitchen, and then appeared in the doorway. "It's time to clean up."

Luke expected Mary Kate to appear behind the girl, but she didn't. "Where's your mom?"

"She's cleaning up in the workout room.

Come on, Michael. You have to clean up, too." She looked at the sawdust on the floor, looking like Mary Kate when she frowned at the sparse contents of his refrigerator. "Where is the broom? I'll sweep."

"In the kitchen closet. But you don't need to do that." Although how he'd get down to the floor to do it, he didn't know.

Shawna reappeared, broom and dustpan in hand, and started cleaning up, chivying Michael along. Luke shoved back out of her way, amused. She was very much the little mother with her brother. Had she always been that way, or was this another result of Kenny's death?

Michael put tools back into their places, pouting. "I don't want to stop already. It's not fair."

"We need some other things before we can do much more," he said quickly. "I'll give your mom a list. We'll work on it again soon. Promise."

"Okay you two." Mary Kate came in quickly, in full mommy mode. "Time to get on home. Is everything cleaned up?"

"I took care of it," Shawna said. She carried the broom and dustpan carefully into the kitchen.

Mary Kate watched her, a slight frown between her brows. Then she seemed to shake it off as she turned to Michael. "Did you say thanks?"

"Thank you." Michael's pout vanished, and he smiled. "I hope we can work some more tomorrow."

"Don't badger." Mary Kate turned him toward the door and gave him a gentle push. "You and your sister take your stuff to the car."

He ran off, and she glanced at Luke. "I hope he wasn't too much of a pain. And that Shawna didn't get in the way."

"Michael was fine. And I barely saw Shawna." He hesitated for an instant. "Are you worried about something? With Shawna, I mean."

He had a quick glimpse of vulnerability before Mary Kate forced a smile.

"No, not at all. Everything's fine." She took a step back. "I'll see you next session. Don't forget to do your exercises."

He hadn't needed the reminder that they were patient and therapist, but maybe Mary Kate had. She had the stiff upper lip down to perfection, just like her daughter.

He grabbed the dangling string and switched off the light. Why did that annoy him so much? He certainly couldn't take on responsibility for anyone else, so he shouldn't be irked that Mary Kate didn't want to confide in him.

His feelings were a mess, and that was the truth. And he didn't see the situation getting any better—not as long as he was seeing Mary Kate every day.

Chapter Eight

If her head would only stop pounding, Mary Kate might have a reasonable hope of getting through the morning session with Luke with her self-control intact. Patience, never her strong suit, was beginning to fray rather badly, and the day had barely begun.

Well, it was at least partially her own fault. She'd stayed up until the wee hours of the morning, making and decorating cupcakes for Michael's class— something she'd forgotten she'd volunteered for until Michael woke up crying about it and reminded her. She'd have to get better organized if she were going to be successful at the whole working-mom thing.

Shawna was percolating a cold and had been up several times, too, complaining that she couldn't sleep because her nose was stuffy.

And the morning hadn't improved matters. Everyone had been out of sorts, the hot-water heater had decided to turn itself off, and she'd finally rushed the children out to the car, feeling as if it hadn't been her best display of motherly patience.

She pulled to the curb at Luke's house and shut off the engine, staring at the azaleas that bloomed riotously at the house across the street. To top it all off, Shawna had continued to insist that nothing was wrong, even though once again she'd walked into the school alone.

She was clenching the steering wheel as if she were bucketing down a mountain road instead of sitting at the curb. She loosened her grip and reached for her bag. Sitting here stewing about it didn't help Shawnie, and none of this was Luke's fault. She owed him her total concentration and her best effort, and that's what she'd give him.

She got out of the car and marched to the door, pasting a smile on her face.

To her astonishment, Luke was there to open the door for her, gripping the walker. "Morning." He stood back to let her in. "You looked as if you didn't want to get out of the car there for a minute."

"It's not that." She set the bag down in the dining room. "I was thinking about some things I have to take care of, that's all."

"Must be unpleasant things, judging by your expression." He moved slowly to the mat where they usually began, then stopped as if unsure how he'd get down to floor level from the walker.

She hurried to take his arm and steady him as he lowered himself to the mat. "Nothing that bad," she said. "Nothing at all, in fact." It would certainly be unprofessional to bring up her misbehaving water heater. "You must have been practicing with the walker. I'm impressed."

"Don't be. It's not exactly a huge accomplishment to walk to the front door and back."

"It is compared to where you were a couple of weeks ago." She had started to kneel next to him when a wave of dizziness hit her. She grabbed the crossbar of the walker, dropping to her knees, willing the feeling away.

"Is something wrong?" Luke watched her. "You're looking white."

"I'm fine."

"Something going on with the kids?"

"They're fine." She snapped the words, then wished she hadn't.

"You're fine, they're fine, everybody's fine. So then why do you look as wrung out as a dishcloth?"

"It's called motherhood." She patted the mat. "Can we please get to work?"

He looked as if he wanted to pursue the subject but decided against it. Wise man. She didn't want to discuss her children with Luke. She still felt a bit raw on the subject of that model car, and now the business with Shawna had added an extra edge.

They're my responsibility, she told him silently. *Mine. I'll take care of them.*

Luke mercifully didn't ask any more questions as they went through the usual routine. She concentrated on the exercises, automatically noting the increase in range of motion and muscle strength. He really was doing well. His natural strength was starting to come into play, whether he realized it or not.

"Okay, that's great." Mary Kate held out her hand to him as they finished the final stretch. "Let's give the bars a try next."

Luke grunted an agreement and caught her hand. She got her feet under her and started to straighten, but the instant she moved, the dizziness hit again, harder this time. The room spun around her, and lights seemed to flash on and off. She was falling, she couldn't help it—

Luke caught her, his arms firm and strong around her. "Hey, easy, what's wrong?" He eased her down to the mat. "Mary Kate, what is it? Are you sick?"

She pressed the heels of her hands against her eyes. "Sorry. Just a little dizzy. Give me a minute."

"Dizzy, why?" His voice was sharp, either with concern or irritation, she wasn't sure which. "Come on, Mary Kate, give."

"I'm fine," she said again. With emphasis. "I just felt a bit light-headed, that's all. I didn't get much sleep last night."

"Why not?" He turned the full force of his dark expression on her. "What have you been doing to yourself?"

"It's nothing." She shrugged, turning to push herself to her feet. But Luke grabbed her before she could make the attempt, pulling her back to the mat.

"You're not getting up until I'm satisfied that you're all right. Come on, M.K., give. Tell me the truth or I'll call your mother."

"You wouldn't." She felt the blood rush to her cheeks.

He smiled a little, as if satisfied. "That brought some color back to your face. Good thing—you were doing a fine imitation of a sheet there for a minute. Now talk, or I get the phone."

"It's nothing." She shook her head, embarrassed and annoyed. "I got to bed late, that's all. I'd forgotten I had to bake cupcakes for the first-grade class."

"Cupcakes?" He sounded incredulous. "You lost sleep over cupcakes? Couldn't you just buy them?"

"I suppose. But homemade ones are better, and anyway—" She shook her head. "This is ridiculous. I lost some sleep, I'm catching Shawna's cold and I didn't have time to eat breakfast this morning." She glared at him. "Are you satisfied? I told you it was nothing."

"You've told me you're too busy taking care of everyone else to take care of yourself," he said. "Do you think you can make it to the sofa?"

"Of course I can."

Luke grabbed the wheelchair and levered himself into it with an ease that would have been impossible even a week earlier. He held out his hand. "Grab hold of the chair. If you feel that you're going to fall—"

"I won't."

Brave words, but she felt her knees shaking under her as she moved slowly beside Luke into the living room and slid down on the sofa. She leaned back, closing her eyes.

"Just let me rest for a minute, and then we'll get back to work."

"You rest while I fix you something to eat. Then we'll talk about whether we get back to work or you call it a day and go home."

She'd argue, but her stomach was growling and her head still throbbed. "I just need a minute. Then I'll fix myself something."

The only answer was the sound of the wheelchair as Luke made his way toward the kitchen. Obviously he didn't intend to listen to her.

A few minutes later she heard him coming back and opened her eyes, trying to look in control.

"Coffee and toast are ready, and the eggs are cooking. You'll have to come to the kitchen, because I'm not sure how I'd get it in here unless I put it in a knapsack."

He was trying to jolly her along, she supposed, but it was so unusual for him to joke about his disability that for a moment she thought she hadn't heard right. She nodded, managing to smile.

"I think I can. Thanks for not telling me how stupid I am to come out without eating." She took the hand he extended and got to her feet.

The floor seemed to tilt slightly, and she couldn't help grabbing his shoulder. If she fell into the chair—

But his shoulder was like a rock. He put his arm around her, holding her against him until the room righted itself.

She drew back, breathless, and found she couldn't meet his eyes. "Thank you."

"It's my pleasure." His voice deepened to a baritone rumble, and for a moment his grip tightened on her arm, as if he'd draw her closer.

Then he was turning away, a faint reddening along his cheekbones the only indication anything had happened.

"Let's get in the kitchen before the eggs burn."

Luke managed to transfer the eggs from stove to plate without incident. He set them down and looked across the kitchen table, studying Mary Kate's face as she buttered a piece of toast. She looked better than she had a few minutes earlier, but the lines of tiredness were still there.

"More eggs?" The scrambled eggs looked a little dry, but he'd never prided himself on his cooking ability. The fact that he'd done it was amazing enough in itself.

"No, thanks. This is plenty." She forked them into her mouth with every appearance of pleasure. "This was kind of you, but I could—"

"Don't bother telling me you could have done it yourself. It's not a sin to let someone else take care of you once in a while, you know."

She glanced up at him, coloring a little. "I suppose not."

Was she embarrassed because for the moment their roles were reversed? Or was she remembering that moment when she'd leaned against him and he'd put his arm around her? He wasn't sure, and maybe it was best not to speculate about it too much.

So his attraction to Mary Kate was still there, ready to rekindle after all these years. That didn't mean it made sense to act on it.

She finished the food in silence and then

leaned back in the chair, cradling the coffee mug in her hands.

"You look better now."

"I feel better. I'm sorry if I didn't seem appreciative. I just don't usually need to be taken care of."

"Or maybe you don't let people do it."

In the essentials she hadn't really changed since high school, he realized. Maybe people didn't, not in the things that mattered. Mary Kate had always tried to take care of everyone.

Some emotion clouded the clear blue of her eyes. "I have to be strong. I'm all the children have now."

"Mary Kate Flanagan Donnelly, you have more relatives than anyone I know, all of them eager to help you."

She raked her fingers through her auburn curls. "It's not that easy. I mean, of course they all want to help. But they have families and lives of their own. I don't want to be a burden."

"You know, you just might be the most stubborn person I know. Wouldn't you help them, if the situation were reversed?"

"Well, of course, but—"

"But, nothing. It's only fair to give them a chance to help you. You're trying to take

Kenny's place all by yourself when you don't need to."

Her smile flickered. "I'm not doing that good a job, I guess, or Michael wouldn't have had to come to you for help with that car."

"Does it really bother you that much?" He reached across the table to snag her hand, holding it warmly.

"I'm trying not to let it." She blew out an exasperated breath. "I know what you're saying is true. It's just not that easy to do. Being a parent can be a scary business even when there are two of you. When you're alone, sometimes it's downright terrifying."

"All the more reason to rely on your family."

She gave him a look that went straight to his heart. "You don't."

He dropped her hand. "That's different."

"Is it?" Her face was troubled. "I know it's none of my business, but I can't help caring. Whatever happened between you and your father in the past, it seems he wants to make peace with you now."

"It's too late for that." Everything in him hardened at the memory of his mother's grief and his own sense of betrayal. "He made his choice a long time ago."

"Don't say that." She leaned toward him

across the table, and the passion in her face and voice startled him. Moved him, in spite of himself. "It's never too late until someone's gone. Then you don't have another chance to say all the things you should have said."

His heart twisted for her pain, and he grabbed her hand again, holding it between both of his. "Don't, Mary Kate. Kenny knew how much you loved him. Don't reproach yourself for anything you said or didn't say."

"I hope——" She shook her head, and a single teardrop escaped her to drop on their clasped hands. "I hope that's right. But that's not the point. You still have time to forgive your father for what he did."

"What if I don't want to forgive him?" His grip tightened on her hand. "He doesn't deserve——"

She reached across to put her fingers over his lips, stopping the rest of that sentence. For an instant his senses reeled at the intimacy of the gesture.

But he knew Mary Kate wasn't seeing it that way. She was just intent on helping him. Taking care of him, the way she did everyone else who came within her orbit. Even when she was dealing with her own weakness, she could still reach out to him.

She took her hand away, looking a little startled at herself. "I'm sorry. If you want to tell me about it, I'd like to hear. It's just been hitting me a lot lately—how little any of us deserve forgiveness, and how much we need it."

For a long moment Luke didn't respond. Mary Kate wanted her words back, but it was too late to recall them. Luke would think she was preaching at him, that she was a self-righteous prig, ready to tell other people what to do.

She wasn't. She was just someone who'd fought that particular battle of the soul very recently, and remembered what it was like to be angry with everyone, including God, including Kenny, for what had happened to her family. She wanted, so much, to help Luke get rid of that debilitating emotion.

You promised to bring good out of even the bad things that happen, Father. If You mean for me to use my grief and anger to help Luke, You'll have to give me the strength to do it, because I'm not sure I can on my own.

Something, some faint lightening in Luke's expression, heartened her. "You don't pull any punches, do you, M.K.?"

"Do you want me to?" Their hands were still clasped. She probably should pull away, but some instinct told her to hold on.

"No, I guess not. We're friends."

Friends. The word echoed in her mind. No matter how much she might tell herself that their relationship was that of therapist to patient, it wasn't true. Their past affected their present, making it impossible to achieve professional detachment. Maybe that was why God had put her in a position to help him.

"As a friend," she said carefully, "I hate to see you hanging on to a grudge against your father, no matter what he did."

He shoved her hands away, half turning from her, and she felt as if he'd pushed her, instead. "You don't know what it was like. If you did, maybe you wouldn't be so quick to forgive."

"Probably not, but—"

"But what?" The face he turned toward her was angry. "I'm a grown-up now? My mother is gone? It's time to let bygones be bygones?"

The harsh words bruised her, but the emotion behind them told her he was hurting much more, holding on to his father's betrayal like a burden he could never put down. Her heart chilled. Was that what lay in

Michael's future—a lifetime of feeling, no matter how irrationally, that his father had deserted him?

No, she wouldn't believe that. Not for her little Michael, and not for Luke if she could do anything about it. But to help, she couldn't hide behind the safety of focusing only on his feelings. She'd have to reveal her own. She'd have to say to him what she hadn't said to anyone else.

"I was angry." Just saying the words felt as if she stripped her soul bare, and she stared down at the worn tabletop, unable to look at him. "Don't bother to tell me it doesn't make sense, because I already know that. I couldn't help it. I was angry at Kenny for dying. For leaving us." Her voice thickened on the words. "And I was angry at God for letting it happen."

"I'm sorry." His voice softened a little. "I know you're trying to help, but it's not the same thing. Kenny didn't have a choice about leaving you."

"We're just as alone. It's just as hard to try and deal with, to raise my children without him. Do you think I don't know how your mother felt? Believe me, I do."

His hand clenched into a fist against the

faded wood, and the knuckles stood out white. "He left her for another woman. He left me to go off and start a new family and he never looked back. It wasn't just being alone or being angry at fate. He betrayed us. He threw us away. You can't know how that felt."

"Maybe not exactly, but—"

He turned away, spinning the wheelchair from the table so suddenly that it startled her. "Not at all." He frowned at her, eyebrows dark and lowering. "Leave it alone, Mary Kate. You're not going to convince me that my father deserves forgiveness."

"It's not about your father." She wanted to reach out to him, but he seemed determined to push her away. "Don't you see that it's not him I'm concerned about? It's you. You're hanging on to all that resentment against him, and it's hurting you far more than it's hurting him."

"I don't let anything about him hurt me anymore. I'm done feeling anything for him." But the bitterness that laced his voice denied the words. "He has exactly what he wants in life. He's a big success—you know that. Well, fine. Let that success be enough for him."

"Don't, Luke." She moved when he'd have

turned from her, grasping his forearm, feeling warm skin and hard muscle against her palm. "Listen to yourself. I know what that kind of anger does to you. Maybe you're stronger than I am, but I know I couldn't live with it. I couldn't move on until I'd figured out how to forgive."

He glared at her, his face still dark with resentment against his father, against her for daring to trespass on his feelings. "Move on? Good advice, Mary Kate. Too bad you're not taking it yourself."

"I am." She'd walk away from him, but she was held by the power of his emotion. "You don't know how far I've come."

"Maybe. But I don't see you moving on. I see you shutting away. I see you so determined to take care of everything and everyone yourself that you won't let anyone else know how much you need help."

"That's not true." It wasn't, was it? She'd been trying to help him deal with his feelings, but he'd turned everything against her.

"It is." His tone was uncompromising. "You came in here this morning ready to collapse because you're trying to do everything yourself. Don't bother to tell me your mother wouldn't have been happy to make those stupid cupcakes for Michael if he had to have homemade, because I won't believe it. You're so convinced you're indispensable that you're trying to make everyone else think the same. Well, you're not."

Stupid tears welled in her eyes, making her furious with Luke and with herself. She tried to blink them away. "Well, if that's true, I certainly don't have to worry about that with you. And as far as you're concerned, I'm perfectly disposable."

She turned her face away, knowing how inane that was. He'd touched a sore point, and he didn't care in the least.

"Come on, Mary Kate." He startled her by grabbing the table to pull himself to his feet. Leaning against it, he touched her cheek, turning her so that he could see her face. "You know that's not true. I really couldn't get along without you. But that doesn't mean I want you wearing yourself out, any more than your kids or your family would if they realized."

"Sorry." She sniffed, reaching up to blot the tears.

Luke got there first, wiping the tears away, his big hand surprisingly gentle. His touch sent warmth shimmering across her skin, and her breath caught.

His fingers spread against her cheek. She found him looking at her with a kind of startled awareness, as if he'd just seen something he hadn't recognized. But whether it was in himself or in her, she didn't know.

He was near, too near. She closed her eyes, as if that would block him out, but it didn't help. She still inhaled the male scent of him, felt the warmth that radiated from his skin, responded when his hand slid back into her hair, tilting her face up until his lips found hers.

Her breath was gone entirely. She couldn't do anything but hold on to his arm, feel his lips on hers, sense a longing and tenderness that flooded through her and met an answering wave of feeling that responded in spite of her best intentions.

Finally he drew back just a little. His breath still touched her skin.

"We shouldn't," she managed to say.

"I know." He traced her lips with his fingertip and then carefully took his hand away, straightening. "I know we shouldn't, but the feelings are there. What are we going to do about that?"

Chapter Nine

Mary Kate still didn't have an answer to that question when she drove Luke to his doctor's appointment the following day. Ordinarily a health aide would do that, but since Luke refused to have one, she'd stepped in. Luckily, Luke seemed just as eager as she was to ignore the whole subject, carefully avoiding any personal conversation.

As for herself, well, she couldn't keep from touching him and still do her job, but she *could* force her will to bring her unruly emotions in line. She couldn't have a relationship with a patient. It was against every rule, as well as common sense, and she wouldn't jeopardize her position.

Fortunately Luke seemed to feel, as she

did, that what had happened was a mistake. It was crucial to regain their equilibrium.

She glanced across the front seat at Luke as she pulled onto Ryland Road, noting the set jaw and the tension revealed in his clenched hands. Maybe it was just as well that they'd gone back to Luke being annoyed with her again.

She nodded to the dashboard clock. "It looks as if we'll be in plenty of time for your appointment." At least the doctor's office was on a quiet road, well away from the downtown traffic.

"An unnecessary appointment." Luke's growl said he still wasn't reconciled to this.

"You couldn't put it off forever." Though he'd done his best to do just that. "The clinic received a rather tart e-mail from the army, asking why they hadn't received a physician's report yet."

"I could have ignored it for another month before they got excited enough to do anything about it if you hadn't been so officious."

"That's me," she said cheerfully. "Officious to the end. I don't see what the big deal is about going to the doctor. He's going to be pleased with your progress."

For a moment she thought he'd ignore her. Then he shook his head. "It's not seeing the doctor I mind. It's seeing other people."

It was past time he faced this issue. "Don't you mean being seen?"

He glared at her, but then gave a short nod. "I guess."

"I can understand your feelings. I think they might be a little exaggerated, though. Plenty of people use walkers and wheelchairs."

She wanted to say that no one would stare, but she couldn't guarantee that, could she? People could be unthinking. Still, Luke had to start getting out more. Maybe today's outing would take some of the apprehension away.

She flicked on the turn signal, slowed and turned right into the concrete parking lot. Mulched beds against the building flamed with color from azalea bushes, softening the starkness of the low, redbrick structure. Several cars were parked in front. She pulled around the side, finding a space at the bottom of the ramp.

"It's a pretty good hike up that ramp. Why don't I get the wheelchair out?" She'd put it in the trunk over his objections.

"No." He yanked at the door handle. "The walker is bad enough."

She knew better than to argue the point. Maybe Luke's stubborn streak was an advantage, if it pushed him to try harder to move forward, as long as he didn't overextend and have a setback. She hurried around the car to position the walker by the door.

When she reached for Luke's arm to help him, he shook her off. She held her breath while he managed the move from car seat to standing on his own. Was he rejecting her help because he wanted to do it on his own? Or because he felt it safer not to touch her? She'd never know.

She followed him up the ramp. *Please, Father, give him strength. If he should fall—* But he didn't, although he was clenching his jaw by the time he reached the top.

Mary Kate scooted around him to hold the door open, hoping she didn't look as relieved as she felt. Inside, a smooth, tiled hallway led to the waiting room. She walked beside him into the room, standing back to let him check himself in. He wouldn't appreciate it if she tried to do it for him.

That accomplished, she headed for two seats together at one side of the room, breathing a sigh of relief when Luke maneuvered the walker to sit down without incident. A young mother sat leafing through a magazine in one seat. The little boy at her feet stopped building a block tower to give Luke a lengthy, unblinking stare, maybe attracted by the metal walker.

Mary Kate frowned at him. He looked four or five—certainly old enough for his mother to speak to him about staring at people. Still, Luke was surely mature enough to ignore a child's stare.

"Do you want something to read?" she murmured, reaching across to the stack of frayed-looking magazines on the blond end table.

"No." Luke's hands clenched the arms of his chair. He couldn't be concerned about the doctor visit, so it had to be the trio of elderly women sitting opposite them.

They glanced toward him and then put their heads together, whispering busily. Mary Kate felt her own tension mount. Maybe the child's behavior was understandable, but theirs wasn't. She could take the walker away, but what good would that do? He needed it, and they'd already seen him use it.

She glanced at Luke. His mouth was set in a straight, hard line that spoke of control clamped down on his emotions. But a tiny muscle twitched along his jaw, and he braced his hands against the chair as if preparing to grab the walker, thrust himself to his feet and walk out.

"Luke—" Her voice was hardly more than a murmur, but he jerked as if she'd shouted at him.

What could she say? That people could behave stupidly, that he had to ignore it? Somehow she didn't think that would help any.

Before she could speak, before Luke could move, one of the women rose and crossed the room to them. Tiny, almost birdlike, she had to be in her eighties. She came up to Luke and put a frail, blue-veined hand on his arm.

If she felt sorry for him, Luke was going to explode. Mary Kate could see it coming and couldn't do a single thing to head it off.

"I just want to say, young man, I know who you are." The elderly voice quavered, and tears welled in faded blue eyes. "And I want to thank you. You served your country honorably, and I'm grateful. We're all grateful."

There was a murmur of agreement from across the room. Mary Kate's throat was so tight she couldn't possibly say anything.

Luke seemed to find it necessary to clear

his throat before he could speak. He sat very straight. "Thank you, ma'am," he said finally. "Thank you."

She'd expected Luke to be wiped out after the excursion to the doctor's office, but she'd also expected him to be, if not happy, at least a little pleased. Not only had the doctor raved about the progress he'd made, but he'd also had the encounter with that sweet elderly woman. Mary Kate had been touched; surely he had, too.

However, Luke didn't show any sign of either fatigue or pleasure on the ride home. When they reached the house, he thudded across the living room to the recliner that seemed to be his favorite seat since he'd deserted the wheelchair.

"Maybe you ought to lie down for a while." She ventured the suggestion, half expecting to have her nose bitten off. She wasn't disappointed.

"Stop treating me like a child. I'm fine where I am."

"Right." She sat down on the sofa. "Since you're so fine, tell me something."

"What?" His frown didn't encourage her.

"You managed well getting there—

frankly, better than I expected. The doctor gave you a good report. Maybe you got a little more attention than you'd have liked, but at least it was positive. So why are you acting like a bear with a sore paw?"

She didn't get the smile she hoped for in response. He shook his head, face tight and controlled.

"Luke?"

"Just leave it alone, okay?"

Frustration got the better of her. "No, I won't leave it alone. Surely you're not upset because that little old lady wanted to express her gratitude to you."

His face tightened. "I guess I don't see it the way you do."

This was his attitude about the medals, surfacing again in a different way. He was convinced he didn't deserve credit for what he'd done when his buddies were still over there.

"I know you're unhappy about being home when your people are still in the line of fire, but no one blames you for getting injured."

There was a flash of pain in his face—masked, but not quickly enough. She'd seen.

"No, maybe I'm wrong," she said softly. "I don't think anyone else blames you for your injury. Except you. That's it, isn't it?"

For a moment, she thought he wouldn't respond. Then his eyes flickered. "You don't know what it was like."

"No. I don't." She had to force the words out. She didn't want to know, didn't want to have images in her mind of how he was injured, any more than she wanted images of her father, her brothers, her husband fighting fire. But denying it wouldn't help him. "Tell me."

Luke was silent, staring straight ahead as if seeing something she couldn't.

Please, Lord. She stopped, not knowing what to ask.

"We were on patrol." He chopped the words off as if they hurt. Maybe they did. "We came under fire from a building we thought was cleared—peppered with automatic rifle fire. When you're in a firefight, the reactions become automatic. I didn't stop to think. I just decided to go in."

Gabe's words about Luke and the football team surfaced in her mind. Yes, of course he'd decided to go in. That was his default action, the one he'd always fall back on in tough situations. He'd spring into action.

"Stupid." His fist knotted on the arm of the recliner. "I was stupid."

"What happened?" She forced the words past the lump in her throat.

"The building was booby-trapped. The explosion went off when I went through the door. It was my fault. Sheer luck that nobody else was hurt or killed."

Of course his first thought would be for his team. "Luke, you took the brunt of it. Even if it was a mistake in judgment, surely that's punishment enough."

His face didn't change. "I charged in without thinking. I was responsible for my people, and I acted on instinct instead of planning."

"I don't know much about it." She picked her way through the words. "But it seems to me that if you were under fire, you didn't exactly have much time to analyze the situation. You did what's in your nature to do."

"My nature, right." At least there was some expression in Luke's face now, even if it wasn't very pleasant. "I've spent my life depending on my strength. That's what I did that day. Now I don't have it to rely on."

She didn't know how to respond. He held on to needless guilt for the way he'd been injured, and he didn't seem to see he had other things going for him besides physical strength.

"Luke—"

"Don't bother, Mary Kate. I know where I stand." He shrugged. "Or sit, I suppose."

"There are different kinds of strength. You must see that. Physical strength isn't the only way you can be strong."

"It's the only way I know."

"No." She leaned forward, wanting to reach out to him, but wary, remembering what had happened the last time they got too close. "That's not true, Luke. You have as much strength of character as anyone I know. That's what makes you a good person, a valuable person, not how fast you can run or how much weight you can lift."

The lines deepened in his face. "That's not how the police department is going to see it. I can't be a cop any longer. Or a soldier. So what does that leave?" He slapped his hands down on the chair arms. "It doesn't matter what the doctor says about my progress. I'll never be who I was before. There's nothing left for me."

Her heart ached for him. "You can't believe that."

"Can't I?" His gaze focused on her finally, dark and intense. "I don't see anything else in my future. And maybe that's what I deserve."

* * *

The doorbell rang persistently, pulling Luke from an uneasy sleep. He pushed himself upright, wincing as he swung his legs from the sofa. He should know better than to fall asleep there, especially in the daytime. It was inevitable that he'd wake with a crick in his neck and a fogged brain.

He reached for the walker. The doorbell was still buzzing, so that meant it probably wasn't Mary Kate. She'd have used her key by this time.

That was just as well. He'd been making too many mistakes with her lately. He shouldn't have kissed her, shouldn't have taken out on her his fears about leaving the house and certainly shouldn't have told her about what happened when he was injured. He only made her share his unhappiness, and given Mary Kate's personality, she'd feel she had to do something to make it better.

He muscled his way across to the door, leaning heavily on the walker. That trip to the doctor had tired him more than he'd expected it to. He'd be lucky to manage a peanut butter sandwich for his supper.

Reaching the door, he flung it open, ready to blast the person making such a racket with the bell. But the words died on his lips. It was Gabe, the golden retriever at his heels, and he carried a flat white box that was giving off the irresistible aroma of pizza.

Gabe held up the box, raising his eyebrows. "My wife and daughter are at a birthday party, and I didn't feel like baching it tonight. How about sharing a pizza?"

Somehow Luke couldn't help but grin, as Gabe's fondness for pizza took him back fifteen years or so. "That better be pepperoni." He stood back to let Gabe and the dog inside.

"What else would it be? Would you believe my wife likes pineapple on her pizza?"

"Hard to understand." He followed Gabe, who was already making his way to the kitchen with the familiarity of long ago. "Be honest with me. Did your sister set this up?"

"Nope." Gabe rummaged in the refrigerator and emerged with a couple of cans of soda. "Much as Mary Kate likes to run things, I managed to figure this out all by myself. I'm glad I caught you home, or I'd have to eat the whole thing." He slid onto a chair and flipped open the pizza box.

"It's a safe bet I'd be home. I don't go out much. Unless your sister makes me, that is."

His mind flickered to the day's outing as he picked up a pepperoni-laden slice of pizza.

"I'll tell you something." Gabe spoke thickly around a mouthful of cheese. "If Mary Kate wants you to do something, you may as well just give up and do it. She's relentless."

He raised an eyebrow. "You sure coming here wasn't something she wanted you to do?"

Gabe shrugged. "Oh, she hinted around that maybe you could use some company, but I'd have come anyway." He glanced down at the dog, stretched out next to his chair. "I guess we have a lot more in common now than we have in a long time."

Luke couldn't argue with that. He concentrated on the pizza, remembering how much he enjoyed it and wondering why it hadn't occurred to him to do a simple thing like ordering in a pizza. He really had been living in a cocoon since he got back.

"Funny, how people drift apart after high school," Gabe went on. "One minute you have everything in common, and it seems like the next, you don't have anything to say to each other."

"True. When I came back to Suffolk the

first time, after my stint in the military, the people I knew from high school were already busy with their own families and jobs. My friends became people on the police force."

And now he didn't have that any longer. He shouldn't have spilled his guts to M.K. that way, but everything he'd said was true.

"It's tough, giving up something you feel you were meant to do." Gabe seemed to be following his thoughts.

"You still have regrets about the fire department?"

Gabe nodded. "It'll always be part of me, even if I'm not fighting fire. You can't change who you are. But I'm content with what I'm doing now."

"Teaching instead of doing?" He couldn't suppress the bitter edge to his voice.

Gabe didn't seem offended at the gibe. "I like feeling I'm training a new generation of firefighters. Even more, the work Nolie and I do with the service animals—" He shook his head. "Never let my father know I said this, but it's even more worthwhile than being a firefighter. We're giving people back their lives, in a way."

"You're lucky. You found two jobs you really cared about." All he'd ever wanted had been the active life he'd had in the military and the police force. He'd told Mary Kate she couldn't understand that, but Gabe could.

"If I hadn't met Nolie, I wouldn't have anything. She saved my life. Literally. If I'd had my way, I'd have gone back onto the fire line even though my seizures weren't under control. Probably killed myself doing it, or worse, another person." Gabe gave him a long, level look. "You're thinking you won't find another job you can do."

Luke stared at the pizza, because that was easier than looking at Gabe. "Maybe I'm not as talented as you. There's nothing else I know how to do."

"You think I knew what I was doing at first?" Gabe grinned. "I made plenty of mistakes, but I learned from every one. You'll figure it out."

Somehow it didn't irritate him as much, coming from Gabe, maybe because Gabe had the credentials. But it didn't convince him.

"Maybe."

Gabe must have heard the rejection in his voice, because he laughed and held up his hands. "Okay, I give up. I won't preach anymore, or you'll think I sound like Brendan."

There's nothing to figure out. That was what he wanted to say, but he didn't. Gabe had nothing but good intentions. He wouldn't return the favor by arguing.

"Well, anyway, that wasn't what I came here for." Gabe took a bite that demolished half a slice.

"You mean you had a motive other than pizza?"

"In addition to pizza," Gabe corrected. "Since you're getting out now, I wanted to invite you out to the farm. Come anytime to take a look around. Come Sunday afternoon. The family's always there for a picnic when the weather is nice. They'd love to see you."

He shook his head. "I'm not much for crowds these days."

"It's just family." Gabe scooped an errant piece of cheese from the tabletop and popped it in his mouth.

"Just family? Come on, Gabe, that's always been a crowd. And now that most of you are married—"

"We've turned into a horde. I know. But think about it, okay? You're welcome anytime. I'll come and pick you up—just give me a call."

"I don't think so, but thanks."

Even as he said it, he realized that the invitation held some appeal. He wouldn't go, but it didn't seem as terrifying a prospect as it would have a few weeks ago.

Maybe that was because being with Gabe felt like old times. Or maybe it was because of Mary Kate and her persistence. Either way, he felt more normal than he had in a long time.

Chapter Ten

"Good shot, Michael." Luke turned his wheelchair and caught the basketball Michael tossed his way. Somehow he'd let the kid talk him into coming out into the driveway for a little one-on-one after they'd worked on the model car.

He tossed it back, and the boy glowed with pleasure when he caught it. "I want to play basketball like my dad did."

"I remember when your dad was on the team in high school. He was a good player." Kenny hadn't had the competitive drive to be a starter, but he'd been solid.

Michael tossed the ball back. Luke dribbled, finding it was actually possible to dribble with one hand and spin the chair with the other.

"Shoot it!" Michael demanded, dancing in

front of him, arms flailing in an attempt to guard.

This wasn't quite the excitement he used to have when he pounded down the floor toward the basket, but he took the shot, finding himself grinning as the ball swished through the bent old hoop above the garage door. He mopped his face with the tail of his T-shirt. The sun glared off the cement driveway, adding an extra level of heat, and Michael, with his fair, freckled skin, was red.

"Let's take a break," he said. "I'm getting pretty hot. Is there any water left in the pitcher?"

"A little bit." Michael rushed to the picnic table he'd helped his mother pull out from behind the garage. He poured a half glass of water and brought it to Luke, holding it carefully in grubby hands.

"Thanks, buddy." He drained it in a long gulp. "I needed that."

Michael hoisted himself onto the bench, apparently ready for a break, too. "We'll be finished with the car pretty soon, won't we?"

He nodded. "A couple more times should do it. I guess you want to take it to school for your project."

Michael shot him a glance and then

looked away quickly. Evasively. "I s'pose," he mumbled.

So there was something else on the kid's mind where the car was concerned. Luke pushed himself a little closer to the table and set the glass down. Well, it wasn't any of his business why Michael was so eager to finish the car. Mary Kate would undoubtedly be the first person to resent it if he tried to pry into whatever was bothering her son.

Not that he would in any event. He didn't mind chatting with the kid about what his dad was like in high school, but he sure wasn't qualified to get into grief counseling, or any other kind of counseling, for that matter.

His mind flickered briefly to his squad, to the long conversations in the quiet of the desert nights about everything from women to jobs to faith. Maybe he'd thought he was helping them, but even if he had, he'd let them down in the end.

Mary Kate and her kids might need help, whether she'd admit it or not, but he was the last man who could provide it.

Michael's feet didn't quite reach the ground, and he swung his legs. He watched them for a moment, and then glanced at Luke. "You're getting better, aren't you?"

"Thanks to your mom and the doctors." Luke grabbed the walker and used it to help him switch from the chair to the bench next to Michael. He wouldn't have thought, two weeks ago, that he'd be doing that much.

"Pretty soon you'll be able to play basketball without using the wheelchair."

The child's innocent words were like a blow to the stomach. "Well, I don't know about that." He tried to keep his voice casual. Playing basketball was probably only one of a long list of things he wouldn't be doing again. "They might not be able to fix me that much."

Michael stared at his sneakers again, tipping the scuffed toes up. "Did you ever hear the story about how some guys brought their friend to Jesus, and they cut a hole in the roof to lower him down?"

"Yes, I remember that one. I always thought they must be pretty good friends." He was afraid he knew where this was going, but he didn't see any way to head it off.

"Jesus made the man better." Michael didn't look up. "In church every Sunday, we pray that you'll get better."

Something twisted in him at that. He should have realized that Pastor Brendan would put him on the prayer list, no matter how many casseroles he turned away. "That's nice of you. I appreciate it."

"Do you ask God to make you better?" Michael asked the question an adult would probably feel too uncomfortable to ask.

"Yes. Sometimes." *But I don't think He's listening to me.* He could hardly say that to a child. "I guess everyone doesn't always get healed the way they want to."

The sneakers stopped swinging, and Michael looked up at him, his small face crinkling as if he were on the verge of tears. Panic swept through Luke. He wasn't capable of dealing with the child's grief. Where was Mary Kate when he needed her?

"Why didn't Jesus heal my daddy? If he could heal other people, why not my daddy?"

He clutched the bench with both hands, the rough wood biting into his palms. "Michael, I'm not a very good person to ask. Why don't you talk to your uncle Brendan? He's a minister, so he knows about things like that."

"I'd rather ask you. 'Cause you got hurt, too, and you wanted Jesus to make you better."

"Yes, but—"

"My daddy didn't want to go to Heaven." The words burst out of him, as if they'd been

dammed up too long. "He didn't! He wanted to stay here with us."

"Of course he wanted to stay with you. He loved you, and he'd have done anything not to leave you." His throat went tight with strain. He wasn't the person to deal with this. He couldn't even cope with his own unanswered questions.

But he was the one Michael was asking, and he couldn't ignore that. *If You're listening, You'd better give me some words, because I sure don't know what to say.*

He took a deep breath, focusing on the kid's face. "Look, Michael, I don't pretend to have all of this figured out. It's really a tough one. Maybe sometimes we can't understand, because we don't know enough. But your daddy's in Heaven now, and he understands why things happened the way they did. Someday we will, too."

Michael looked as if he wanted to argue that one. But he couldn't, because his mother came toward them from the porch, carrying a tray with a pitcher and glasses.

"Lemonade," she said, her voice light.

But blue sparks shot from her eyes when she looked at Luke, leaving him in no doubt. Mary Kate had heard his feeble attempt to answer Michael's questions. And she was absolutely furious with him.

Mary Kate set the kids' empty glasses back on the tray. The smile she'd had clamped on her face for the past ten minutes felt as if it were frozen there, but anger bubbled hotly behind it. When she got Luke alone, she'd tell him just what she thought of his interference.

"Okay, you two. It's time you went over to Grammy's house. Luke and I need to work some more."

Shawna nodded, getting up, but Michael's lower lip came out in a pout.

"I don't want to go yet. I want to play basketball with Luke some more."

"Well, you can't." She hated the way that sounded, so she reached out to ruffle his hair, trying to make the smile a bit more genuine. "You've been here for quite a while, but now you have to leave. Say thank-you to Luke for helping you."

It might be the last time—or at least the last time she left Michael alone with him. He didn't have the right to talk to her son about his father's death. No one did.

"Thank you, Luke." Michael slid off the

bench and scuffed his toes in the grass. "I wish I could stay longer."

"Sorry, buddy, but I have work to do, like your mother said."

At least Luke had sense enough to back her up in that, but it didn't begin to take the edge off her anger. They stayed in frozen silence until Shawna and Michael were well down the block on the way to her mother's, and then she swung on him.

"You had no right to do that."

"I know." He didn't pretend he didn't understand. "But if you'll listen to me—"

"I heard you—" grief grabbed her throat "—talking to Michael about Kenny."

"Look, I didn't want to." Luke propped his elbows on the picnic table, looking up at her. "How about sitting down so we can talk about this?"

I don't want to. That was what she wanted to say, but it sounded petulant, even to her. She slid reluctantly onto the bench across from him. "There's nothing to say."

"I repeat, I didn't want to talk to him about it." Frustration tightened his face. "Michael brought it up. I told him he should ask Brendan his question, but he asked me. He thought I would understand." His tone was bleak.

She clenched her hands together. "What question? What did he ask you?"

"He wanted to know why Jesus didn't heal his daddy."

For a long moment she couldn't speak. She could only struggle to hold back the tears.

Luke reached across the table to put his hand over both of hers. "Look, I'm sorry. He seems to have the idea that I'm kind of in the same boat, so I should know the answers." He shook his head. "I don't. I told him that. I just tried to reassure him as best I could."

She sucked in a shaky breath, staring at his hand covering hers. It was lean from his long struggle, but still strong. She couldn't let herself rely on that strength.

"I don't mean to sound unreasonable. Believe me, I know how persistent Michael can be." She tried to smile, but it was a dismal attempt. "Sometimes I think he was born asking why. But dealing with those kinds of questions is my job." *Not yours.*

His fingers tightened a little. "I know. But he didn't ask you, Mary Kate. Don't you wonder why?"

That hit her like a blow, and all she could do was stare at him. She tried to yank her hands away, but he held them tightly. She clamped her lips together. She would not fall apart in front of him.

"I'm sorry." His voice was soft. To do Luke justice, this seemed to hurt him, too. "I know it's none of my business, but I can't help seeing it. You're so determined not to let anyone, especially the kids, see your pain."

"I can't." The words rasped her throat. "They're children. I'm the grown-up. I have to protect them."

His hand moved absently on hers. Comforting, as she would comfort one of the children.

"You're really good at that stiff upper lip of yours. Trouble is, it's rubbing off on them."

"No." She shook her head, went on shaking it. She had to deny it. "That's not true."

"Isn't it? Shawna's exactly like you, determined to take care of everyone. If something's bothering her, she's not going to admit it. Again, like you."

The memory of Shawnie, walking into school alone, clutched at her heart.

"And Michael, hiding the car from you because he didn't want to hurt you." Pain roughened Luke's voice. "It's none of my business. I accept that, but I can't help seeing what's right in front of me."

"No, I guess you can't." She drew another shaky breath, knowing tears weren't far away. She pulled at her hands and this time he let go. She put them up to her face. "I'm letting them down. Just like I let Kenny down."

There was a brief, startled silence, lasting long enough that she could hear the persistent chatter of the wrens in the birdhouse near the porch.

"What makes you think you let Kenny down?" he said finally.

She wouldn't cry. She wouldn't. But the tears were already slipping down her cheeks, and she had to wipe them away with her fingers.

"I should have taken better care of him. I was too wrapped up in the kids to see that something was wrong. Why didn't I?" She tried to stop the words, but once her guard was released, they poured out in a torrent. "I'd have taken the kids to the doctor at the slightest symptom, but I didn't even realize anything was wrong with him. If I'd noticed, if I'd pushed him to go to the doctor, have a checkup, maybe they'd have found it earlier, maybe he wouldn't have died, maybe—" She broke off with a sob that she couldn't control.

Luke just sat, listening, until she ran down. Until she dropped her hands, palms down, on the table, as exhausted as if she'd been running.

"How could you have realized something was wrong sooner if Kenny didn't even see it?"

She shook her head tiredly. "I don't know."

"You don't know because it's impossible." Luke clasped her hands again, very gently. "Think about what you just said, and tell me how you'd respond to anyone else who believed that."

She knew, even without thinking. "I'd say that was foolish. I'd say nobody could have known and—" She stopped.

"And what?" He was implacable. He wouldn't let her off the hook until she'd admitted it.

"And nothing would have made any difference."

"So why can't you do the same for yourself?"

All the arguments welled up in her. *Because I'm the one who takes care of everyone, because I'm the responsible one, because I should be able to fix everything.*

She didn't say anything. She just confronted all her reactions and knew how ridiculous they were. She took a breath and realized she felt freer than she had in a long time.

Lord, were these words from You?

"I'm supposed to be your therapist," she said softly. "Not the other way around."

She managed to look at him, and found a softness in his eyes that shook her. She felt an emotion in return that was so strong it frightened her. She'd known the attraction existed. She'd been prepared to deal with that.

But this was much more than just attraction. This was caring and affection and a whole host of feelings that she very definitely didn't want to face.

Mary Kate pulled into the driveway that circled the clinic and the hospital several days later. She stole a glance at Luke as she parked in one of the handicapped spots near the hospital entrance. He was clutching the armrest, and he didn't let go until she'd come to a complete stop.

"You know, if I make you that nervous, you might think about getting strong enough to drive again yourself," she said, her voice tart.

He blinked. "Sorry. It's not you, exactly. It's just—"

"You like to be in control."

"I guess."

"Your mother's car is automatic. The way you're improving, I think you might—"

His hand closed over the door handle. "I'm not into wishful thinking."

"It's not wishful thinking." Shaking him was not an option, but she hated running up against that stubborn streak of his, especially when it limited him. "It's perfectly reasonable to think that eventually you'll have enough control to drive. A car with hand controls would allow you to drive right away."

"No. If I can't do the real thing, I'd just as soon walk." He pushed the door open and swung his legs around.

Exasperated, she slid out, shut the door a little too hard and went around to lift the walker out for him.

By the time they reached the hospital entrance, she'd gotten herself under control again. Really, this was ridiculous. She wasn't the sort of person to let her emotions get the better of her. It seemed everything she felt had been out of kilter lately, especially where Luke was concerned.

She held the door for Luke to go through. "If the brace and the canes work out, you'll soon only need the walker occasionally." She nodded to the right. "The orthotics department is down here."

He moved along beside her without comment. Because he didn't have anything to say, or because he was apprehensive about this new step in his recovery? She wasn't sure but decided not to push it.

They reached the office, and Luke was swept off by the technicians who were eager to work with him but probably too polite to mention his military service as the reason. For once she had nothing to do but find a seat and watch.

Over the next half hour, while they fussed over the proper fit of the brace, she found her apprehension rising. How was he going to take this? The doctor thought he was ready, but Luke might not agree.

At least he wasn't arguing with the techs the way he usually did with her. An unwelcome thought intruded. Maybe he'd have been better off all along with someone he didn't know as well or feel so free to balk.

Common sense asserted itself before she could go too far down that path. If she hadn't intervened when she did, Luke would have continued turning physical therapists from his door. She was the one who'd gotten him started, and she was right to be pleased about that.

She watched, heart in her mouth, as the techs hoisted Luke to his feet, helping him balance with two canes. His face was tight, lips set, betraying nothing, but she knew him well enough to read past that. He wanted this, and he was afraid to want it.

Please, Lord. This would be such a big step, in every way, for him. Please, let this work.

She held her breath as he steadied himself. His tension flowed across the room, striking her like a physical blow. She'd worry later about what it meant that she knew so well what he felt. Now she could only clench her hands on her knees and pray. *Please. Please.*

He moved his legs, testing, getting used to the feel of the braces that helped support him. Then, slowly, very slowly, he took one step and then another. He looked up, smile blazing across his face at the triumph. But the smile wasn't for the person who helped him. It was for her.

Before she could identify the emotions that rocketed through her, he'd looked away, concentrating on the instructions he was getting.

He moved forward, stopped, turned, balancing carefully, lurching a little so that her heart was in her throat. And then he moved again, walking away from her.

Walking away from her. His smile had shown the sense of achievement she'd been longing to see. That was what she wanted, wasn't it?

Of course it was. And the sense that he really was walking away from her—well, that was her function. She was supposed to help him become independent, even when it took him away from her.

She fought the unwelcome feelings throughout the rest of his session and even while she listened to the final instructions for his use of the braces and the canes. She'd best pay attention, especially to the cautions about doing too much too soon, because otherwise Luke would probably insist on doing just that. She'd had the sense all along that something could happen to turn all that stubborn will of his into getting better instead of fighting against healing. Judging by his expression, this might be it.

Predictably, he wanted to use the canes to walk out to the car. It took the orthotic tech's arguments, added to hers, to dissuade him.

Finally, giving in to persuasion and threats, he took the walker, letting her carry the canes.

She pushed the door open, and he moved through it to the top of the ramp. He paused there for a moment, tilting his head back to catch the rays of the sun. Then he looked at her. "Feels good."

Her throat tightened as she realized he wasn't talking just about the sunshine. "Yes," she managed. "Yes, it does."

She was startled when he lifted the walker and went swiftly down the ramp. Faster than he ever had before, faster than he should have, probably. He beat her to the car and leaned against it, grinning with triumph, as if they'd been racing.

"Okay, you won. No need to gloat."

She unlocked the car, opening the back door to set the walker and the canes inside. She shouldn't let him see the effect that wide, easy grin had on her. It turned him into someone else, the boy he'd been once, a long time ago.

When she closed the back door, she realized he hadn't made any move to get into the car. He stood, arm resting against the roof, as if enjoying the sense of towering over her.

"Tell you what—I feel like celebrating. Let's go out to dinner."

It was so unexpected that she couldn't say a word. For an instant she felt sixteen again, being asked out by the boy she'd dreamed of for too long. She looked up at him, acceptance trembling on her lips.

Then cold common sense swept in. It wasn't particularly comforting, but it was what she'd grown used to.

"I'm sorry, Luke. That—that wouldn't be appropriate. I can't go out on a date with you."

"No?" His eyebrow lifted. "But we're old friends. And we did that before."

I know.

"That doesn't make a difference. I'm your therapist. I can't date a client."

"Well, I don't insist upon it being a date. I just want to celebrate. Can't we have a nice meal while we discuss the future of my therapy? You can pay your own way, if it makes you feel better."

What he said was logical enough, but all her instincts warned her of the danger of being out alone with him.

"I don't think that's a good idea." She tried to sound cool, professional, as if she didn't care.

Unfortunately, it didn't seem to be working, because he was still looking down at her with that quizzical smile, as if waiting for a better explanation.

Well, he wasn't going to get one. "Shall we go home?"

He got in the car, but she sensed more was coming. Sure enough, once they were on the bypass, he turned toward her.

"So, if I accepted Gabe's invitation to his house for a picnic, and you were there, would that be against the rules?"

She clenched the wheel. And her jaw. "I don't see how anyone could object to that. Gabe's your friend."

"And if I accepted your mother's invitation to go to church with the family, that would be acceptable?"

She sighed. "Luke, please let it go. Please."

"Sure. Consider it dropped."

But he was smiling, and she suspected she hadn't heard the end of the subject.

Chapter Eleven

M ARY KATE sat back on her heels and looked with satisfaction at the impatiens, their pink and lavender faces nodding along the side of her house. "You were right, Mom. They look beautiful here."

"I think they'll do well." Siobhan planted her trowel into the damp earth and lifted another pot of impatiens from the tray she'd dropped off unexpectedly on Saturday morning. "They'll like the afternoon shade."

"Kenny always put geraniums here." Taking care of the yard and flower beds had been Kenny's province. Last year she'd still been too raw from his passing to even think about planting flowers.

"Geraniums like more sun." Her mother smiled, her eyes crinkling. "Naturally I never said that to Kenny. I didn't want to be an interfering mother-in-law."

"Interfering? You couldn't interfere if you tried. Help, yes."

"Some would say there's a fine line. Your father, for instance." Warm laughter laced her voice.

"You know Dad's just teasing you."

"That's his favorite thing," Siobhan agreed.

Mary Kate stared at the plant she held in her hands, then slid it out of the plastic pot and pressed it down into the waiting hole. She wasn't quite sure how to bring up the subject that had been lurking in the back of her mind, waiting for an opportunity.

"You knew Luke's parents for a long time."

"Knew them, yes. Not really well, but as you say, for a long time."

"Were they ever happy together?" Maybe, if she understood what his folks had been to each other, she'd understand Luke better. Maybe it would even help her know what to do with her inappropriate feelings.

Her mother sat back on her heels, wiping her damp forehead with the back of her gardening glove and depositing a smear of mud in the process. "It's always hard to guess what's going on inside someone else's marriage. I had the feeling that Ruth rather resented the fact that his business occupied him so much. You don't make a success like his without putting a lot of hours into it."

"You mean he neglected his family."

"I didn't say that. A lot of women would have been proud of his drive, maybe even jumped right in to help him run the businesses. Ruth wasn't like that." Her mother shrugged, going back to the planting. "I'm not saying one of them was right and the other wrong."

"Luke feels his father deserted them." And he was still hurting about it, after all these years.

Her mother didn't respond immediately. The steady movement of her trowel was somehow soothing. Mom had a way of immersing herself in whatever she was doing, as if planting a flower or sewing on a button was an important task.

Maybe it was. A line from an old hymn sounded in her mind. *Let all our work be praise.*

She'd like to cultivate the serenity that would allow her to feel that about every task of her day, instead of unraveling with worry when things didn't go her way.

Her mother tamped down the rich earth around a flower. "I suppose that's true enough. Phillip was the one who left, and it's natural that Luke has some resentment."

"Not some. A lot." It was on the tip of her tongue to tell her mother about the issue of Luke's father helping to pay for his therapy, but that fact wasn't hers to tell.

"Ruth was a difficult woman in some ways." A line formed between her mother's brows. "After Phillip left, she wouldn't let anyone help her except Luke. She put everything on him— all her feelings, all her worries about the future. He was just a boy, too young to cope with that."

Some emotion she couldn't quite identify slid through her. Was it fear that she might do the same thing with her children? Or just the recognition that she understood what Ruth had felt, even if she didn't condone what she did?

"It's still affecting Luke. His father has called several times, but Luke refuses to speak to him. I can't help but think it would be better for Luke to get past it. To forgive."

"You're worried about him." Siobhan cut right to the heart of what she was trying to say. "I thought he was doing better."

"He is, physically. He graduated to braces and canes, and he's navigating pretty well with them. He's starting to interact normally with the kids, with Gabe. But he still feels guilty about leaving his men in the battle zone, and he's holding on to his anger with his father like a—like a crutch."

"Maybe that's what it is. It lets him focus his negative feelings on the past instead of confronting what has to be an uncertain future." Her mother reached across to pat her hand. "I understand you worrying about him. It's only natural, but his emotional health isn't your responsibility."

Wasn't it? She couldn't dismiss it that easily, but Mom would never understand unless she leveled with her.

"Mary Kate?" Her mother pressed for an answer. "Is there something more you want to tell me?"

She couldn't help a wry smile. "Are you ever going to stop knowing your kids' minds better than they do?"

"I hope not." Siobhan squeezed her hand.

"Luke isn't just any patient. I mean, we have a history. That's what let me get him started on his therapy to begin with, but now—"

"Now what?"

Her mother would probably sit there on the grass all afternoon, waiting for her to come out with it. But how could she admit she was attracted to him? More, cared about him?

"It's...well, it's different. The other day, after he started on his canes, he wanted me to go out with him to celebrate."

"I can understand that. He was probably euphoric. He'd have wanted to celebrate no matter who he was with."

"Not like this. He wanted me to go out to dinner with him. I can't do that. It's too much like a date. It wouldn't be ethical to date a client."

"I see." Siobhan sounded as if she saw far too much. "Is that the only reason?"

She bit her lip. "No." She had to push the words out, and she didn't dare look at her mother's face. "I have—we have both felt some, well, attraction to each other. I'm sure it's nothing," she added quickly. "I mean, we once dated in high school, and now we're in a situation that's fairly intimate and it's just—"

"You're attracted to each other." Siobhan said it briskly, as if it was perfectly normal. "There's nothing wrong with that, but I agree, it would be inappropriate to act on it while you're his therapist. But you won't always be his therapist."

"No." She didn't want to admit to the bleakness she felt at the thought of not seeing Luke on a regular basis.

"You could date then. No one could criticize that."

Panic swept through her. "I'm not sure I want to date Luke or anyone else. How can I? I have the children to think of. I feel disloyal to Kenny just talking about it."

"Oh, Mary Kate." Her mother's voice was warm with sympathy. "It's been over a year. You can't stop loving Kenny, but that doesn't mean you can't ever love anyone else."

Siobhan didn't understand. Mary Kate wasn't sure she understood herself.

"I don't know if I have it in me to love someone else in that way. How will I ever know if I can? What if I made a mistake? I can't hurt Shawnie and Michael by exposing them to more heartache."

Her hands twisted together in her lap until her mother took a firm grip on them.

"Honey, I don't know all the answers. But I think, when the time comes, God will show you the way. Just trust in that and ask Him to show you the answer."

Her heart was too full to speak. All she could do was nod and try to hold back the tears.

"Mommy, get the ball!"

In response to Michael's shout, Mary Kate bent to stop the soccer ball. She kicked it back toward Michael and the swarm of little Flanagans who had turned the lawn at Gabe and Nolie's farm into an improvised soccer field. Nolie had provided bushel baskets for the goals, and they were as happy as if they had uniforms and a regulation field.

She strolled toward the group of adults gathered under the big oak tree. Sunday dinner was a Flanagan tradition, and she loved it when the weather was nice enough to turn it into a picnic at the farm.

She dawdled, not especially eager to be drawn into a discussion with Dad about the Phillies' chances this year. Truth to tell, she was just happy to be here and soak up the serenity. She needed a little peace to get her rebellious emotions under control.

She actually came close to telling her mother how she really felt about Luke the other day. That was something she didn't want to admit even to herself.

She glanced back toward the children. The

game had changed—now Shawna was teaching them to play Follow the Leader. Trust Shawnie to entertain her little cousins endlessly, even though she often lost patience with her own brother.

"Hey, Mary Kate." Brendan loped up to throw an arm around her shoulders. "Worried that the game is getting out of hand?"

"No, not at all." She leaned against Brendan, affection welling in her. Brendan had always been more brother than cousin since he'd come to live with them when his parents died. "Just thinking how good it feels to see them all playing together. And next year you'll have one to add to the bunch."

"Right." Brendan's face softened, as it always did at the mention of the expected baby. "I don't think he or she will be playing soccer so soon, though."

"I guess not, but he or she will grow up knowing there's a lot of family around to play with. And a lot of love." *Thank You, Father, that my children have this.*

Brendan squeezed her shoulders. "Missing Kenny?"

"No, not really. Just thinking that it's almost as if he's here somewhere, off talking baseball with Dad or shooting hoops with Gabe."

Brendan looked at her closely. "Does that feeling comfort you?"

She shrugged. "I'm not daydreaming, if that's what you mean. I know it's best to stick with reality."

"It's natural enough to…" Brendan paused, glancing at the car that was pulling up where the farm lane petered out in front of the house. "Who's Gabe bringing?"

She followed his gaze, and her stomach lurched. Gabe was coming around his car, reaching out to open the passenger door. But he was too late. The door swung open, and Luke swiveled to put his legs out.

Luke. Of course, she knew Gabe had been after him to come to dinner, but she'd never imagined he'd actually accept the invitation.

She detached her arm from Brendan, hoping he hadn't noticed any involuntary reaction on her part. She'd better get herself under control, before one of her other observant relatives guessed what she was feeling.

Gabe handed him the two canes that must have been in the backseat. At the sight, any thought of hanging back fled. What was he thinking? She hurried across the grass to him.

"Hey, M.K., look who finally agreed to show his face." Gabe clapped Luke's shoulder, nearly hard enough to knock him off his precarious balance.

"I see. Welcome, Luke." She shut the door once he was clear of it, relieved to see that the walker was in the back, also.

"Hi." He gave her the slow smile that never failed to send ripples along her nerves.

She might be safer if he returned to the habitual frown he used to have. How was she going to keep her feelings secret when he could affect her so easily?

"Don't you think you should use the walker? The ground is uneven, and walking on grass is more difficult than pavement or wood floors."

His smile didn't fade, but it might have stiffened a bit. "I'm fine for the moment. I brought the walker in case I need it later."

She put her hand on his arm, and it felt like steel through the sleeve of the denim shirt he wore. "Luke, I really think—"

"I'm sure you do." There was a glint of determination in his eyes. "You're not my therapist today, Mary Kate."

"I can't turn it off that easily."

"You'd better try, because I don't intend to obey any orders. Not unless you're telling me to come to the table."

She managed to smile. Obviously she'd have to humor him. "Well, in that case, maybe you *had* better come to the table. I think I see the appetizers arriving."

She should make some excuse to move away, but that would be rude. She was the logical person to smooth his way into the family group. She'd make sure he was occupied and then she could slip away.

On the other hand, maybe he didn't need her help. He made his way to a lawn chair and once he was balanced, held out his hand to her father.

"Mr. Flanagan. It's good to see you again, sir."

"Luke, sit down." Her father beamed. "Glad you came, son. Mary Kate said you weren't getting out much, but it looks as if you're getting around pretty well now."

"I'm making progress." He eased into the chair. "Thanks to Mary Kate. She's a good physical therapist."

Her dad's eyes twinkled. "She's always been good at telling other people what to do."

"Hello," she said, nettled. It really wasn't fair for her own family to take Luke's side. "I'm standing right here."

"Sure you are, sweetie." Her father chuckled. "You're just too easy to tease."

Before she could find an answer, she heard a shout from Michael. Deserting the game, he came running over, followed by Shawna.

"Luke, Luke." He threw himself at Luke, and for a second she thought the chair would collapse under both of them, but Luke reached out a strong hand to catch him.

Michael threw his arms around Luke's neck in a throttling hug. "I was wishing you would come, and you did."

"Your uncle Gabe invited me. He said you have a lot of fun here."

"We get to play with our cousins and see the animals. Hey, wanna see the animals? Come on, I'll take you."

Shawna had reached them by now. "He wants to have something to eat first, don't you, Luke? I'll bring you some iced tea. And some fruit. There'll be cookies later, but Grammy says we can't have them until after we eat real food."

"No, animals first." Michael tugged at Luke's hand.

"Hey, you two, give the man room to breathe." Her father's voice was laughing.

"It's all right." Luke put an arm around

Michael and patted Shawnie's hand. "Tell you what. You tell me all about the animals, and Shawna can tell me about what we're going to have to eat."

Mary Kate stood where she was, watching them. Michael leaned unselfconsciously against Luke's knee, as if they'd been friends all his life. Shawnie's face was animated as she chattered away about all the food Grammy and her aunts had brought. And Luke listened to them as if he really cared.

Her heart twisted. It was the way they used to chatter to Kenny, telling him all about their day, knowing he wanted to hear every little thing.

They'd missed that. Despite having all the attention from her, from family, they still missed that kind of relationship. For some reason she couldn't understand, they'd latched on to Luke.

This was what it had been like with Kenny, but Kenny was gone. With an odd clarity, she realized she hadn't accepted that until this moment.

Luke shook his head at the dessert plate Mrs. Flanagan was holding out temptingly.

"It's the best cherry pie I ever tasted, but I can't possibly eat another bite."

"Then I'll wrap some up for you to take home." Siobhan Flanagan whisked off toward the farmhouse, apparently to do just that. She went quickly up the ramp to the porch. Obviously Gabe and Nolie, with their service animals, were used to providing for people who needed that.

Gabe, stretched out next to him in a lawn chair, chuckled. "You may as well not fight it. If Mom's determined to feed you, she will." He shut his eyes, leaning his head against the canvas back of the sling chair, obviously content.

For an instant Luke felt a twinge of resentment. Gabe had it made—a lovely wife and child, a beautiful place to live, meaningful work to do. He just as quickly shoved the feeling aside. The golden retriever sleeping at Gabe's side might look like the family pet, but he was much more than that. Gabe would probably spend the rest of his life dealing with his seizure disorder, and for all Luke knew, he might miss being a firefighter more than he'd ever let on.

Gabe was one person who might understand his concerns about the future. But if he was tempted to bring it up, the words died on his lips. Gabe's eyes were shut, his breathing slow and even.

Smiling a little, he glanced around. The drowsiness seemed to be affecting all the men, lounging in the shade after they'd cleared the picnic tables from the huge meal. The children had deserted the sunny field to gather around Joe Flanagan for a story. Joe obviously enjoyed his role as patriarch of such a large clan. Luke tried to imagine his father in such a role, but he couldn't. Phillip Marino had never made family and faith the center of his life, as Joe so obviously did.

As for him, well, he couldn't imagine it for himself, either, and that was why this attraction he felt for Mary Kate and the affection that was growing for her children scared him. And that was why he'd come today.

He had to see Mary Kate on more neutral territory. He'd told her she wasn't his therapist today, and that was what he'd meant. He needed to clear his mind about what they were to each other. About what they could be.

He stretched his legs out in front of him, still faintly surprised when they obeyed him. A week ago he wouldn't have entertained the thought of a relationship with anyone, especially Mary Kate, with two kids to consider. How could he possibly be responsible for kids?

But moving to the braces and canes had begun to make him feel that things were possible again—a job, a meaningful life. Or maybe it was Mary Kate who was doing that. She'd certainly worked hard enough at it.

That was why he had to see her as something other than his therapist. He wasn't sure, and he needed to be.

Gabe roused at a call from his wife, wide-awake in an instant, fireman that he was at heart. "She has work for me, no doubt." He shook his head and moved off toward the farmhouse. In a moment his place was taken by Brendan.

"I thought Gabe would never give up this chair." He glanced toward the porch, where his wife sat in the porch swing, talking to Nolie.

Luke nodded toward the pair, blond hair and dark close together as they talked. "You can't take your eyes off your wife, can you?"

Brendan grinned. "I'm just so...overwhelmed. I'm going to be a dad. How am I going to manage that?"

"Copy your uncle, I'd guess." He nodded toward Joe, who had a lapful with the youngest while the others gathered around his knees.

"You've got a point there. I couldn't go wrong doing that. Neither Claire nor I had what you'd call good relationships with our own fathers, so we look to Joe for guidance."

That was a thought he'd have to mull over if he really let himself entertain the idea of a relationship with Mary Kate. Always assuming, of course, that she felt anything for him other than friendship, the concern of a therapist for a patient and that leftover attraction. He knew instinctively that a relationship with her required a lot more careful handling than anything he'd experienced before.

Brendan glanced at him. "Have you given any thought to what you're going to do with yourself long-term?"

That was a question he didn't want to hear, much less answer. He didn't begin to know. A few weeks ago, he hadn't foreseen anything other than turning into a hermit. Now...

He shrugged. "Not sure. I don't know that the police department will have much use for me, even with these." He gestured with the canes.

"If you want to talk about it anytime, give me a call." Brendan smiled. "If you can manage to think of me as a pastor instead of a second-string wide receiver."

"I..." It wasn't that he had trouble thinking of Brendan as a minister. It was that he didn't care to talk about something that was still such a question mark in his own mind.

He looked up and saw Mary Kate moving toward him across the lawn. Her gaze met his, and an unspoken message seemed to pass between them.

"You two get enough to eat?" she asked.

Brendan groaned. "You should know better than to ask that around here."

"Why don't you organize a game for the kids? That'll get your blood moving. And be good practice for you."

"You could do that."

"I'm going for a walk with Luke." She smiled at Luke a bit tentatively. "I know I'm not your therapist today, but would you like to try out a stroll on the grass?"

He nodded, reaching for the walker that was propped against the picnic table. "Good idea. Maybe it's time to switch to this thing, though."

She waited until they were several feet from Brendan before giving him a look of mock astonishment. "You actually did that without putting up a fight."

"Hey, I'm not stupid. I'm not going to risk scaring the kids by toppling over."

"Well, I don't think you'd scare them, but thanks, anyway." She nodded toward the barn, a typical Pennsylvania Dutch structure, huge, lofty, painted a warm red. "Think you can make it that far?"

He nodded. "Sure thing. And thanks for coming to the rescue."

"You looked like Brendan might be bugging you a bit."

Had he? Or did she just read him that well? She was looking at him with a question in her eyes, but he wasn't ready to talk about his future with her, either.

"I was afraid he was going to bug me about why I didn't go to church this morning."

They started up the easy slope to the huge barn doors. "A good question."

Mary Kate grabbed the metal handle and shoved the door across. It ran easily, but then he'd expect anything Gabe took care of to work well.

He stepped inside, onto wide, aged planks. Stalls ran along the sides, empty now, and the loft above was down to the last few rows of hay bales. Sunlight filtered through the door in the loft and dust motes danced in it.

"It's a peaceful place," he said quietly.

She nodded, sitting down on a rough

wooden bench that looked as if it had been made from wood left over from building the barn. "It is. Like a church sanctuary when you slip in during the day."

Was that what Mary Kate did when life threatened to overwhelm her? He sat down next to her, not sure he should ask.

Her head was tilted back, and she seemed to stare, bemused, at the shaft of sunlight crossing the barn loft. "So why didn't you go to church today?"

"I didn't have a ride." That wasn't the reason, and he knew it.

"There are only about a hundred people who'd have been happy to pick you up. Try again."

He linked his hands around his knee, frowning at the floor. "Let's just say I'm not on good terms with God right now and leave it at that."

"Not a chance." She turned toward him, and he felt the focus of her intense gaze. "Do you think I don't know that you're angry with God? You may as well say it."

"What's the point? That won't change anything." He suspected she wasn't letting it go. In his effort to keep the focus off his future, he'd opened another can of worms.

"I know it seems that way now, but—"

"Don't tell me you know how it feels, Mary Kate. You can't."

"Can't I? After Kenny was diagnosed, I went through a period of rage so intense it scared me." Her voice was very even, but he thought it took a struggle. "And again after his death. I kept trying to hide it, as if I could hide from God."

She was hurting. Because of him, because she wanted so much to help him that she'd bring up things that hurt her.

"You don't feel that way now." Maybe there was a question in that.

"No. Not after I talked it out with Mom." Her voice softened. "She pushed me to get it all out, and later my sister did, too. I think it took that—their pushing, and time and raging at God when it got the better of me."

"So you decided to try the same thing on me." A few weeks ago he'd have been furious at her interference. Now it didn't seem to bother him.

She nodded. "I just wanted to say that, well, eventually I came to feel that God understood my pain even better than I did."

"Does He?" He couldn't entirely suppress

the tightness in his voice. "Right now He just seems very far away to me."

She didn't say anything. Just looked at him, waiting, with a world of concern in her face.

"All right, I'll say it. As long as I was in control I didn't spend much time leaning on God. And now that I'm not in control, I think He should fix it. Not very reasonable, is it?"

"Maybe not reasonable, but human." Her lips tightened. "That being in control—it's an illusion. We're never really in control. We just think we are."

A wave of empathy swept through him. He wanted to wipe the sorrow from her face. Wanted to make everything better for her. He reached out to brush a strand of hair back from her cheek, his fingers lingering against the warmth of her skin.

"I'm sorry," he murmured. "I wish—" He shouldn't do this, but she drew him in ways he didn't understand. He turned her face toward his.

Her eyes widened, lips parting on a breath. And then she drew back. "Don't, Luke. Please. It's not right."

He didn't want to stop. "I thought we decided you're not my therapist today."

"I don't think my boss would see it that way. And even if he never knew, I'd know. I can't have a romantic relationship with a client." Color came up in her cheeks at the words.

Maybe that answered some of his questions. He stroked her cheek lightly and then reluctantly pulled his hand away. "You won't be my therapist forever, will you?"

She shook her head, eyes questioning.

"I can wait." He pulled himself to his feet with the walker. "Maybe I should let Michael show me the animals."

Because if I stay here with you any longer, I might forget all the reasons why this is impossible.

Chapter Twelve

Mary Kate slid down into the therapy pool, welcoming the warm water. Spending time in the therapy pool herself was one of the perks of working at the clinic. Luke was already in the pool, along with Frank Morgan, who was talking away to Luke as if he'd known him for years. Going to the family picnic seemed to have broken through some of Luke's reserves. He'd put up only a token resistance to sharing his pool therapy. Frank's blue eyes sparkled as he told some anecdote about his therapy.

"Come on, now, Frank," she said. "You know you enjoy your therapy. You're my favorite patient, remember?"

He grinned. "Thought maybe I'd been replaced by this young fellow."

"Nobody could ever replace you," she said.

But Luke's gaze met hers, and she could feel warmth flood her cheeks. Was he thinking, as she was, about those moments in the barn on Sunday?

Flustered, she tried for her normal session tone. "Okay, you two, let's pick up the pace. You can walk a little faster than that."

The two men reached the far side of the pool, then turned and started back, facing her, and Luke's gaze crossed hers again.

In an instant she was back in the barn, sitting next to him, feeling the mix of guilt and hope she'd felt then. There'd been a promise of something between them, and even though she'd felt guilty just for thinking of it, she couldn't help being drawn to the possibility.

Mom believed God would make Mary Kate's course clear when the time was right. She could wait. Would wait. Nothing was clear right now except that her heart was confused.

Another thing was clear, also. Whether or not Luke admitted it, he was getting better, and her job at the moment was to take him as far as he could go. After that, well, she supposed she'd see what happened.

"All right, let's try some leg lifts. Hold on to the side of the pool, please."

"She's a slave driver, that one," Frank said. "She'll never let you get away with anything."

"I've noticed." Luke's eyes were warm.

She would not let herself respond. "Ready? Raise your outside leg gently. Let the water help lift it."

"Feels as if I'm back in the army again," Frank said. "Calisthenics, every single day, that's what we did, right up to the time we went overseas."

She held her breath, half expecting Luke to tense up at the reminder, but he looked at Frank with what seemed genuine interest in his face.

"Where were you stationed?"

"Where weren't we?" Frank lifted his leg energetically. "Started out in France and worked our way east."

"You were in World War II, then. Mary Kate mentioned something about it, but I didn't believe you were old enough."

She breathed again at the light tone of his voice, half losing track of the conversation as she directed their exercises. Frank was doing exactly as she'd hoped, his cheerful manner and matter-of-fact talk about coming home from the war engaging Luke.

Exercising together kept both of them going longer than either of them would have alone, probably. Luke had been by himself too much, and each time she managed to get him around other people, he moved a little farther out of his shell.

Maybe, with Gabe's help, she could come up with some other things that would show him he could live a normal life. That was what he needed—the assurance that what had happened to him wasn't the end. Certainly Frank was doing a good job with him in that respect.

"Yes, I can remember when there were fifty or more of us marching in the Memorial Day parade," Frank said as they finished the cool-down sequence. "Not like that now, though. Not so many WWII vets left. Still, I'll be there."

"Riding in the back of a convertible, I'll bet," Mary Kate said. "Okay, you can get out now and dry off." She moved to the ramp, just in case either of them needed help, but they moved up side by side.

"Well, you'll be there this year." Frank patted Luke's shoulder. "Be mighty glad to see some of you young fellows in the parade."

Luke stiffened, turning so cold in an instant that it was a cold breeze on her skin. "Afraid I won't be there."

Don't let him hurt Frank, Lord. Please.

"Hey, all the guys take part in the parade." Frank looked bewildered. "It's like paying tribute to the ones who didn't make it."

"Maybe Luke's going away that weekend," she said quickly, handing Frank his towel. "I'll be watching for you though. Be sure you wave to my kids, okay?"

"Will do," Frank glanced at Luke. "You change your mind, just get in touch with me. I'll tell you where to be."

"Right, thanks."

Luke's face was tight, but Frank didn't seem to notice. He moved off toward the dressing room, waving over his shoulder.

Mary Kate waited until she was sure he was out of earshot. Then she swung toward Luke. "You didn't have to be so short with him. He was just being nice."

"I'm not going to be in any parade." He grabbed his towel, slinging it around his neck.

"The Memorial Day parade is a tradition, you know that. You grew up watching the veterans march in it, just as I did." And decorating the graves at the cemetery, too, but it probably wasn't safe to mention that.

"It's not for me." The words dropped out like ice pellets. "I have no intention of appearing in my uniform like this." He grabbed the walker and stumped toward the locker room.

She tried to swallow her disappointment. Every time she thought Luke was making progress, another roadblock surfaced, usually where she least expected it.

Luke stood at the kitchen counter, balancing on only one cane while he poured a mug of coffee. That was progress of a sort, as he was sure Mary Kate would be quick to point out.

Except that Mary Kate didn't seem to be in any hurry to get here today. Her scheduled time wasn't until ten, but he'd grown accustomed to seeing her turn up early, sometimes carrying a loaf of her mother's cinnamon bread, to share coffee before they started the therapy. And since she'd already informed him that she'd have to leave promptly after their session because the children had only a half day of school today, he'd say she was sending him a message.

The atmosphere had grown considerably cooler since the incident with the elderly vet at the therapy pool. He stood at the counter, looking out the kitchen window at the rhododendron blooming against the garage, and frowned a little.

He hadn't shown any disrespect for Frank Morgan, so why did she find it necessary to scold him as if he were a rude kid? Sure, she was right about one thing. He was getting better. He'd gone farther than he could have imagined a few short weeks ago.

But there were things he wasn't prepared to do. Why couldn't she accept that?

The doorbell rang. He set the mug down, sloshing a little coffee on the countertop, and reached for the second cane. Mary Kate arriving? She'd probably have let herself in by now.

When he reached the living room he could see who stood on the porch, and he automatically stood a little straighter. Lieutenant Pete Ragan of the Suffolk Police Force peered through the glass, one hand up to shade the glare of May sunshine.

Okay. He took a firm grip on the canes, back straight. At least he was dressed, shaved and walking with the canes instead of slumped in the wheelchair, the way Mary Kate had found him that first day. Stiffly erect, he strode toward the door, if he could call it striding when he had to use canes to support every step.

He swung it open. "Lieutenant Ragan. Good to see you, sir." And why are you here? He'd made it clear, the first week home, that he didn't welcome company, even from his buddies on the force.

"Marino." Ragan studied him for a moment. "You don't look half-bad. Some of the boys made it sound like you were at death's door. Glad to see they were wrong." He managed what was, for him, a genial smile.

Luke held the door open and stood back while Ragan sidled in. Fate had given the man a drooping, lugubrious face that made him resemble a basset hound on the verge of tears. Combined with his slight stature and hesitant manner, it caused some people to underestimate him. Luke had never made that particular mistake. Ragan ran his department with an iron will and a fierce determination that it be the best.

"Have a seat, sir. How are things downtown?"

"Not bad." Ragan sent a mournful glance

toward the sofa and settled instead on the bentwood rocker. "I hear you're coming along pretty well yourself."

It took an effort to keep a smile on his face as he sat down in his usual chair, sliding the canes on the floor out of sight. Ragan had heard from whom? Had Mary Kate been meddling again?

"Have you been talking to someone I know?"

Ragan shrugged. "Ran into an old buddy of mine down at the VFW. Frank Morgan. Had some good things to say about you."

Not, apparently, including his refusal to participate in the Memorial Day parade, or Ragan wouldn't be looking at him with approval.

"We had some therapy together." He kept his tone neutral.

Ragan leaned forward, elbows on the chair arms. "I figured it was time we had a talk about your future."

His jaw tightened, and tension knotted his hands into fists. "My future."

"With the department."

Ragan frowned, and Luke steeled himself. If he was about to be offered retirement, he'd like to have been a little better prepared for this conversation.

"So?" Ragan's brows lifted. Obviously he expected a response. "You figure on coming back? When the army lets you go, that is."

Truth time. He took a brief look at how far he'd come. At how much farther he could expect to go. He wanted to rage at God, at the lieutenant, at his own stupidity for charging in without thinking. But what good would any of that do?

"The army docs say they don't know how much use of my legs I'm going to get back." It took more effort than he'd thought possible to get the words out evenly. "If I can't be one-hundred percent, I won't be on the street again. I won't let someone else's life depend on me if I can't hack it."

Ragan studied his face for a long moment. Then he gave a slow nod. "Fair enough. Either on the street or in the office, you can still be a cop. When the army lets you go, there'll be a place waiting for you, either way." He stood, holding out his hand.

Luke took it, still trying to process Ragan's words. The offer was more than he'd expected, but not what he'd hoped for. "Thank you, sir."

"Glad you're back, Marino." Ragan waved him back when he would have gotten up.

"That's all I came to say. You call me when you're ready."

When he was ready. But if all the future held was a lifetime behind a desk, would he ever be ready for that?

"That's enough for today." Mary Kate took out her frustration on the exercise mat, rolling it into a tight cylinder. "You're not concentrating."

Luke got to his feet, using the canes. He glanced at her, but he didn't deny the charge. "I have something on my mind."

"What?" She shook her head instantly. "I'm sorry. It's none of my business."

"Maybe it is, in a way. I had a visit from my old boss."

"From the police department?"

He nodded, and she tried to decipher his expression. She couldn't.

"What did he say?" If Luke had just learned he'd never be a police officer again, it would go a long way toward explaining his lack of attention.

"Asked me if I wanted to come back." Luke didn't meet her eyes. "The bottom line was, if through some miracle I get back to normal, I can have my old job back."

"And if not?" She hurt for him, but she kept her voice level.

"He offered me a desk job." His tone made it clear how he felt about that.

"That's not so bad, is it? At least you'd still be a cop, even if you weren't out on the street."

"Pushing papers around."

She just looked at him for a moment. Why did he have to be so blind? "If you don't want a desk job, don't take it."

He looked up, startled, at the snap in her voice. Well, good. At least she had his attention.

"Honestly, Luke, sometimes I want to shake you. You have a lot to offer, and there's a world of things you could do, even if you never got a bit better than you are today. Why don't you see that?"

He didn't say anything, and his face was so stolid that she couldn't tell whether her words had angered him or not. Finally he shook his head. "I guess maybe you see more than I do, Mary Kate. I wish I had your faith."

Her heart hurt with the need to reach him. But she couldn't. He was the only one who could convince himself that his life was still worth living.

The thunder of feet on the back porch

warned her, and she turned toward the kitchen in time to see Michael erupt through the screen door.

"Hi, Mommy. Hi, Luke. Grammy said we could come over and see if you're finished yet." He sent Luke, who'd followed her to the kitchen, the melting look that usually persuaded people to do what he wanted. "I thought maybe Luke had time to work on the car a little bit."

"Not now," she said quickly. Luke had enough on his mind right now. "You two go out in the backyard until I'm ready to go. And behave."

Shawna, standing at the door behind her brother, nodded. "Come on, Michael. Don't be a pest."

Michael went out, but his high voice floated back through the screen. "I'm not a pest. You are. You're a pest and a scaredy cat."

Whatever Shawna answered, she was far enough away that they couldn't hear it. She tried to manage a smile as she glanced at Luke. "At least he's gotten past the stage of using potty words when he's trying to be annoying. Sorry about that."

"No problem." Luke turned to the counter,

fiddling with the coffeemaker, presenting a broad, uncompromising back to her. "You can go now, if you want."

"Thanks." She bit off the word. "I'll put the equipment away first."

She stalked back to the workout room before she could give in to the temptation to begin the conversation about Luke's future again. Arguing with him wasn't going to do any good, and she wasn't sure what would.

Chapter Thirteen

She began cleaning up the equipment, putting it away automatically, trying to keep her mind on each task. And not on Luke.

She wanted so much to help him. She couldn't, not in the healing that really mattered.

Please, Lord. Luke needs to turn to You. He has to find acceptance, and I don't know how to show him that. I have enough trouble with that myself.

She was almost finished when she heard a hoarse shout from the kitchen. She dropped the five-pound weight she was holding and raced toward the kitchen. If Luke had fallen—but she'd have heard it, wouldn't she?

She burst through the kitchen door. No Luke, but the back door stood open, and she could hear Michael's shrill cry from the yard.

Heart thudding, she raced across the kitchen, through the door, onto the porch. *Please, Lord, please, Lord...*

It took a moment to understand what she was seeing. Luke, full-length on the grass, struggled to get to his feet. Michael stood under the tree in the corner of the yard, wailing. And Shawnie lay crumpled in a tangle of broken branches on the ground.

She sprinted to her child, dropping to her knees beside the small form. "Shawnie, are you all right? Talk to me."

She had to pull broken branches away to see Shawna's face. Blood streamed from a cut on her forehead. Her cheek was scratched, her eyes dark with shock, but she was conscious and moving.

"Michael, stop that!"

Michael stopped in mid-shriek and looked at her, blue eyes wide in a white face. "She fell, Mommy. The branch broke and Shawnie fell."

"I see that. Now go in the kitchen and bring me a couple of clean dish towels from under the sink. Right now."

"Yes, Mommy." He turned and ran.

"Is she all right?" Luke's voice was so tight she almost didn't recognize it.

"I'm okay." Shawna tried to push the

branch away, her face set in a stubborn look that announced she wasn't going to cry, no matter what.

"You're going to be fine." She had to keep her voice calm. She was the mom. She had to be calm. She pulled the branch free. "Does anything hurt besides your head?" She ran her hands along blue-jeans-clad legs, praying.

"I'm okay, Mom. Don't make a fuss. I'm not a baby."

"You're also not okay." But at least there didn't seem to be anything other than the gash on her forehead. "We're going to have to see the doctor about that cut."

Michael bolted across the yard to them, a wad of clean dish towels in his hands. She took them, focusing on using them to apply pressure to the cut.

Luke had gotten to his feet. He must have seen Shawnie fall and tried to get to her. Satisfied that she had pressure on the cut, she glanced at him.

"Are you okay?"

"Yes." He cut the word off. "Can I do anything? Call someone?"

She put one arm around Shawna, holding the pad against her forehead as she helped her to her feet. "Think you can walk as far as the car, sweetie?"

"I can walk." Shawna's stiff upper lip was operating overtime.

She sent Luke a harried look. "I'm going to have to take her to the doctor—stitches, I'm afraid. If you'll keep Michael for me..."

"No." Luke's face darkened with some emotion she couldn't name. "I can't."

She blinked. "It will just be for a little while, until I can reach my mother to pick him up."

He shook his head. "I can't be responsible for him. Don't you get it? I saw Shawna, but I couldn't get to her. I can't be responsible for anyone else."

She had to talk to him. Had to make him see that this wasn't his fault. But Shawna was bleeding, and Michael looked as if tears weren't far off. The kids came first.

"Michael, get in the car." She led Shawna, still protesting, toward the car.

Luke needed her. But her kids came first. That was the bottom line. Her kids came first.

Mary Kate stood in the doorway of Michael's room that evening, listening to the sound of his quiet breathing. The glow from the night-light was enough to show the mound in the covers, the glint of red hair against the pillow and one small hand outflung. For these few moments, he was her baby again.

Resisting the impulse to go in and pat him, she closed the door quietly and crossed the hall to Shawnie's room. The light beside the twin bed was on, and Shawna sat propped up in bed, a book open on her lap.

"Not sleepy yet, sweetie?" She sat on the edge of the bed, patting her daughter's leg.

Shawna put the book aside, shaking her head. The bandage stood out, stark white against her red curls.

"Does your head hurt?"

"It's okay."

There it was again, the quick denial that anything was wrong. Her heart ached. Luke had been right. Shawna had developed a stoicism that was far beyond her years. The question was, what was she going to do about it?

"The doctor said it would probably feel a little sore tonight. It's okay to admit that." She tried a teasing note. "You don't have to act like a superhero, you know."

Shawna's long lashes veiled her eyes. "I know, Mommy."

That was a little heartening. For the past year, Shawna had been convinced that calling her anything but "Mom" was baby stuff.

"You know, I miss hearing you call me Mommy once in a while," she said softly. "No matter how big you get, in some ways you'll always be my little girl. Just like sometimes I'm Grammy's little girl."

Sitting here in the quiet bedroom just reinforced that feeling. She remembered the day Kenny put the crib together, talking about the baby. They hadn't wanted to know ahead of time if it was a boy or girl, so they'd decorated the nursery with a Noah's Ark border on pale yellow walls.

But Shawna had outgrown the Noah's Ark theme, and now Mary Kate faced her child's troubles alone. The cut head and stitches she could handle. That was what Luke had failed to understand. The run to the hospital for stitches, scary as it was, still had an element of familiarity for any mom of two active kids. When she'd been growing up, it was a rare month when someone in the Flanagan family didn't damage himself or herself in some way.

No, it wasn't the physical injury that scared her. It was the emotional pain that Shawnie was doing such a valiant job of hiding—that was what wrung her heart.

And she had to find some way of handling it. Alone. Kenny had never seemed so far away. So dead.

"Aren't you going to scold me for climbing Luke's tree?"

"Do you know you shouldn't have done it?"

"Yes, Mommy." Shawna hung her head. "I was trying to show Michael I wasn't scared. That was dumb."

"Well, if you know that, then I guess I don't need to tell you."

Shawna nodded, her face still troubled.

She breathed a silent prayer for wisdom and put her hand over Shawna's. "I know something is wrong at school, sweetie. I really wish you'd tell me about it."

Shawna's lips tightened. "There isn't anything you can do, Mom. Mommy," she amended.

Her heart twisted. "Maybe not, but I'd still like to hear about it."

Shawna shrugged, seeming determined to hold the words back. Tears gleamed in her eyes, and she blinked rapidly.

"Casey says she doesn't want to be my friend anymore. And she got some of the other girls to say they don't want to be friends, either."

"Shawnie, I'm so sorry. That must really hurt." She wanted to rage at the unfairness of it, but that wouldn't help Shawna in the least.

Shawna's mouth firmed. "Today Casey acted like maybe she wanted to be friends again, but I'm not going to be friends with her again, not even if she wants me to."

Lord, give me wisdom. "You and she have been friends for a long time, since kindergarten, I think. It would be a shame to lose that. Sometimes people can start a quarrel and then not know how to get out of it."

"Casey started it." Shawna's anger spurted out. "She should tell me she's sorry before we can be friends again."

"Honey, holding on to a grudge doesn't hurt anyone but yourself." Her mind flickered briefly to Luke, desperately hanging on to the grudge against his father. "If you want to be friends again, you might have to forgive first. Will you think about that?"

The blue eyes that met hers swam with tears. "Okay, Mommy."

Answering tears formed in her eyes. "It

hurts when someone you care about lets you down. It's okay to cry about it."

Shawna swiped at her eyes with the back of her hands. "Crying is for babies. You hardly ever cry, even about Daddy dying."

The words pierced her heart like a knife, taking her breath away. "Oh, honey, that's not true. I've cried a lot about Daddy." She let the tears spill over onto her cheeks. "I guess I should have let you and Michael see that, but I thought it might make you feel scared if you saw me crying. Maybe we should remind each other of that sometimes, okay?"

Shawna nodded, and then lunged forward to wrap her arms around Mary Kate fiercely. "I love you, Mommy."

"I love you, too, baby." She held Shawnie against her heart, her cheek against the bright hair, and let healing tears flow.

It was nearly an hour later when she finally came into the living room, feeling drained but relieved. She and Shawna had gotten past something major, at the cost of a few stitches. If it hadn't been for the accident, how long might it have taken her to realize the truth of what Luke had said about Shawna? And why could he, a relative stranger, see what eluded her?

She glanced around the slightly cluttered living room, taking comfort from the familiar. This could sometimes be a rough time, once the children were in bed and the house was quiet. A time when loneliness could creep in and blossom into grief if she didn't hold it at bay.

As she reached for the remote, intending to fill the silence with something, anything, the doorbell rang.

Some family member, coming by to see how Shawna was?

But when she drew aside the window curtain, Luke stood on her front stoop. For a moment she was so startled she froze. Luke, here? Luke, who never went anywhere unless she badgered him into it?

She pulled the door open quickly. "Luke?" She couldn't entirely keep the amazement from her voice.

"I came to see how Shawna is." His tone was clipped, his face tense, as if he braced himself for bad news.

"But how did you get here?" She shook her head, the answer obvious. A taxi waited at the curb.

Luke jerked a nod toward the cab. "He'll wait for me." He raised an eyebrow. "May I come in?"

"Yes, of course."

Flustered, she stood back to give him room to enter. He moved slowly, but he was using the canes instead of the walker.

"Please, sit down." She banished a faint regret that she hadn't used the few minutes she'd had to tidy the living room. She whisked two toy cars off the recliner that had been Kenny's favorite chair.

He sank down, setting the canes aside and leaning toward her. "Shawna?"

"She's fine. Really, she is. I thought the doctor might just put a butterfly bandage on it, but she decided to put in a couple of stitches, just because of where the cut is."

His face relaxed visibly. Guilt took a bite out of her. Why on earth hadn't she thought to call him?

"I'm so sorry." She sat down in the rocking chair opposite him. "I should have called to let you know that she's all right."

He shook his head. "You don't owe me any apologies, Mary Kate. I understand. You were completely taken up with the kids."

That was true enough, but somehow it only

increased her sense of guilt. "If I'd called you, you wouldn't have had to come over."

"Didn't you think I could?"

"I think you can do just about anything you set your mind to. I'm just surprised this is what made you do it."

"It was my tree, after all." A glimmer of humor showed in his dark eyes. "Maybe I was afraid you'd sue."

"If I blamed other people every time one of my kids got hurt, I'd spend my life in court. It's amazing what two normal, healthy kids can manage to do to themselves."

"There was nothing normal about what happened today. When I saw Shawna on that branch and knew it wouldn't hold her—" He stopped, jaw tightening. "I don't know when I've been so afraid."

"I understand." She was unaccountably touched. "That's what turns mothers' hair gray. It's a wonder my mom didn't have a headful of gray hair by the time she was thirty, raising the bunch of us."

That diverted him from the guilt he seemed to be feeling, as she intended. "Now that I think of it, the Flanagans did rush off to the emergency room fairly often."

She nodded. "It was usually Ryan, trying

hard to do what the older ones did and breaking a bone or getting a black eye in the process. I guess that goes with being the youngest."

"I wouldn't know." His face darkened a little, and she remembered what he'd said once, about being jealous of their big, noisy family. Coupled with Mom's comments about what his mother had been like, it gave her a bit more insight into what made him tick.

She leaned forward, reaching out impulsively to touch his hand. "If you're feeling guilty because it was your yard and your tree, please stop. It was just kids being kids. Apparently Michael called her a scaredy cat, and she had to prove she wasn't."

He shook his head. "I don't feel guilty because it happened at my place. I feel guilty because I saw it happening and I couldn't get there in time to help."

"You tried." Her voice went soft, and she saw him again, stretched out in the grass where he'd fallen, trying to reach her child.

"But I didn't succeed." His jaw clenched. "I let her down."

"Luke, it wasn't your fault." She should have realized he would blame himself.

He shook his head. "I was there. I couldn't help her. It feels like my fault to me."

"You're making too much of this." His sense of responsibility was part of what had made him a cop and a soldier, but he was letting it skew his vision. "I don't care if you'd been a world-class sprinter, you couldn't have reached her."

"Maybe not, but it feels like a pretty solid indication that I shouldn't be assuming responsibility for anyone."

That was what he'd meant, then, when he'd refused to watch Michael for a few minutes. Her heart hurt for him.

"You're talking about how every parent feels when a child gets hurt the first few times." She hesitated. Did that make it sound as if she thought he had, or would have, that kind of relationship with her kids? "You get over it, because if you didn't, you'd overprotect your kids and keep them from growing up."

He shook his head. "I'm sorry, Mary Kate. You don't know how sorry." Some emotion crossed his face, so fleeting that she couldn't identify it. "But it doesn't change what I feel, what I know. I can't put myself in a position where I'm responsible for someone else's safety and happiness."

She knew what Luke was really saying. He was saying that, whatever they might feel, they didn't have a future.

Chapter Fourteen

Luke leaned back in the pew, glancing toward the stained-glass windows. Rain might be pouring against the panes, but the atmosphere inside Grace Church was warm and bright, alive with music, friendly faces and a message he'd needed. The song they'd sung at the beginning of the service, about the sweet spirit in this place, had been true.

He didn't quite know what instinct had driven him to get up early, dress and call a taxi to take him to morning worship. Maybe it was the sense that he'd hit bottom, emotionally, in the moment he'd seen Shawna fall.

Odd. He'd certainly been more depressed during those long weeks in the hospital when he hadn't been sure he wanted to keep on breathing.

But the moment he'd realized he wasn't going to reach Shawnie in time had given him a clear-eyed vision of what his future could and could not be. Now the problem was to accept it.

Whatever had brought him here this morning, the instinct had been right on target. Brendan's sermon had been as conversational as if he sat around a kitchen table with friends. He'd talked about hearing God's voice in the whirlwind, about finding peace in the midst of chaos.

The words had reverberated in Luke's heart. He knew all about the whirlwind in the form of the sand that swirled up in the desert, getting in your eyes, your ears, distorting everything so that you didn't know where you were or who your enemy was.

He'd known the chaos. Now he sought the peace.

He stood for the closing hymn, balancing himself against the pew in order to open the hymnal. When he looked up, glancing across the pews, he met his father's gaze. He looked away, more confused than angry.

Brendan would probably say that peace would elude him as long as he held on to the anger in his heart. But it was deserved, wasn't it? How could it be right to ignore the harm someone had done?

When the final Amen had been said and sung, the organ burst forth in a joyous peal. People began turning to their neighbors, greeting each other, the buzz of conversation competing with the organ's notes.

He was suddenly as eager to leave as he'd been to come. Too many people, too much noise, too many competing emotions jostling through him. He had to get home to sort it all out. But as he reached the end of the pew, a small body came squirming through the crowd to him.

"Luke!" Michael's face lit with a smile that the most hard-hearted would find impossible to resist. "I wanted to talk to you, and you're here."

"I'm here," he agreed. "How are you doing? Is Shawna better?"

"She's okay." Michael shot a quick glance over his shoulder. "Listen, you still want to finish the car with me, don't you? Mommy said maybe I should ask Uncle Gabe to help me with it, but I said you'd be sad if I didn't let you."

"That's not exactly the way it went." Mary Kate reached her son, catching him by the shoulders. "Michael, it's very rude to rush through where people are trying to walk."

"But I had to see Luke. I was afraid he'd leave if I didn't hurry. And he wants to help me with my car. Don't you, Luke?"

Mary Kate met his eyes, harassed, and shrugged a little. "I'm afraid this is just like asking if someone can come to dinner when the someone is standing right there. I was trying to explain to Michael that now that you're getting better, you might not have time to work on the car with him."

She was giving him an out, if he wanted to take it. He should do just that, but how could he when Michael was looking at him with such trust in those big eyes?

Don't trust me, he wanted to say. *Don't depend on me, because I might let you down.* But he couldn't.

"It's okay." He'd like to wipe the wariness out of Mary Kate's eyes, but he couldn't do that, either. "We can finish it up in one session. Michael, you come over when your mom's there some time this week. All right?"

"Yeah! I knew you'd say yes. I'm going to tell Uncle Gabe."

Michael went squirming off through the crowd again, but he didn't have to go far. A whole phalanx of Flanagans was bearing down on them. Shawna reached them first and grabbed her mother's hand.

He nodded to her. "How's your head?"

"It's okay." Shawna wiggled, pulling on Mary Kate's hand. "Mommy, can I go talk to Casey before she leaves?"

"All right." Mary Kate smiled, shaking her head a little as Shawna rushed off. "I guess trying to teach my kids manners at the end of the worship service isn't such a good idea."

He looked after Shawna, who'd caught up with a friend. They had their heads together, giggling over something. "She seems none the worse for wear."

"She's fine. Having stitches has increased her popularity at school for some reason." Her gaze met his, and again he saw that wariness. "Are you sure about Michael? You don't have to be bothered with it if you don't want."

"I promised him. And I can't do much damage with you right there."

"Luke—" She stopped, biting her lip. Maybe she figured this wasn't the time to teach him anything, either.

Hard. It was hard just to stand there, not giving anything back to her. But if he started, it would be worse in the long run. They could never be anything but friends, if that. Mary Kate was defined by her kids, and he couldn't possibly take on that kind of responsibility.

The crowd was thinning out. He took one step toward the door, and then Siobhan and Joe Flanagan reached him. Siobhan put her hand on his arm, so that he couldn't escape without shaking her off. Even in his need to get out, he couldn't be that rude.

"Good morning, Mrs. Flanagan. Joe."

"It's so good to see you out at church this morning. We'd have been happy to pick you up, if you'd just let us know."

"Thanks, but I didn't have any trouble getting here." They didn't need to know he'd come by taxi and planned to go home the same way.

"Well, it's too wet out for a picnic, so we're having dinner at our house today. Why don't you come? We'd love to have you."

He kept a smile on his face with an effort. It wasn't going to be easy to preserve a polite distance from Mary Kate if her family kept inundating him with invitations.

"That's nice of you, but I already have plans." Eating a frozen dinner and watching the Phillies on television constituted plans, didn't it?

"If you can't make it this week, at least promise you'll join us for the Memorial Day picnic next weekend. Unless you're going to be with your father, of course."

"No. I'm not." Not that his father would ask him, in any event.

"That's settled, then." She patted his arm before releasing it. We'll plan to see you after the parade, then."

His smile slid, despite his best efforts. Had Mary Kate told them about his reactions to being in the Memorial Day parade? No, of course she wouldn't do that. She looked just as awkward as he felt.

She took her mother's arm. "Come on, Mom. We don't want to keep Luke standing here talking if he has plans. We can make arrangements about the picnic some other time."

He took advantage of the moment to turn away, nodding toward Gabe and Seth and their families. "I'll see you later. Have a pleasant afternoon." He started up the aisle before anyone else could stop him.

Memorial Day was a week away—so it had been over a month since Mary Kate forced her way into his life. Somehow it seemed both longer and shorter at the same time.

He reached the door, nodding his thanks to a teenage boy who held it open for him. Incredible, that she could have become so important to him so quickly. And just as incredible that it would soon be over.

Give it another week, and he could move into going to the clinic a couple of times a week for his therapy. Maybe schedule it at a time when Mary Kate wouldn't be there. They'd drift apart, and eventually the ache in his heart would go away.

It was for the best, but he'd be awhile convincing himself of that.

Michael's voice, light and high, sounded from the workroom. Mary Kate paused in the act of putting lunch dishes away in Luke's kitchen, listening. She couldn't hear the words, but she could interpret the tone of voice. Michael, usually a little shy with people he didn't know well, was chattering away as if Luke had always been part of his life.

She didn't understand, hadn't understood from the beginning, why her son so was drawn to Luke. The initial attraction of the wounded soldier was natural enough, but it had always been more than that. It was as if

Michael instinctively recognized in Luke someone who would be a friend.

The low rumble of Luke's response touched a chord in her heart and she struggled to deal with it. Neither of them had intended to develop feelings for the other. It had seemed inappropriate on so many levels. But it had happened.

And just as she had begun to feel something might eventually be possible between them, Luke had slammed the door on it. Why was it so difficult for him to understand that he had a great deal to offer, no matter how fast he could move?

"Mom!" Michael poked his head around the door frame. "Hurry, come and see the car!"

"I'm on my way." Drying her hands on a tea towel, she followed her son into the workroom.

The space no longer had a dusty, forlorn look. Man and boy working there together had changed it, although they certainly hadn't cleaned it up.

"This place could use a good cleaning." She whisked the tea towel at the bench top and it came away grimy. "How can you work in here?"

Luke actually smiled for the first time in

days. "Just like a woman. Men don't need clean when they're working with tools, do they, Michael?"

Michael positively danced with excitement. "Look, Mom, look. But don't touch it. The paint has to dry for twenty-four hours before anyone can touch it," he added importantly.

The car, gleaming red with a silver racing stripe, sat in the middle of a piece of newspaper on the workbench. The overhead light was focused directly on it. They'd staged this, she realized, and her reaction had to be just right.

"Wow," she said it slowly and reverently. "That's absolutely beautiful. I can't believe you did all that. It's a masterpiece."

"It is. And I did most of it, Mommy. Luke just helped and told me how to do it."

She bit back the urge to remind him to thank Luke. The two of them had developed their own relationship and she knew instinctively that intruding on it would be wrong.

"That's wonderful, Michael. I'm so proud of you."

And proud of Luke, too, although she could probably never tell him that. He'd accomplished as much as Michael had in bringing this project to completion. He'd become a different person from the man she'd met that first day, and her son had been one of the keys to that transformation.

"Daddy would be proud, too. Wouldn't he?"

She suppressed a pang. "Yes, he certainly would be proud of you."

Michael stood at the edge of the table, his hands twisting together. "Twenty-four hours is a long time to wait."

"Maybe it would go faster if you didn't stand there looking at the car," Luke suggested, and she heard the smile in his voice.

"Good idea." She took Michael's shoulders and turned him away from the table. "Why don't you go out and shoot a few baskets while Luke and I talk? I'll be ready to leave in a little bit."

"Okay, Mommy." He rounded the table and stopped in front of Luke. "We did good."

Luke held up his hand for a high five. "We sure did, buddy."

"I bet I can make five baskets." Michael dashed for the door. "I'll come and tell you if I do."

She waited until the screen door had slammed behind him before she turned to Luke. "Thank you. You've done a wonderful thing for him. Something I didn't even realize needed to be done."

He shrugged, putting the lid back on a can of enamel. "I enjoyed it. He's a great kid. You should be proud of the way you're raising both of them."

"Learning from my mistakes, anyway," she said. "And that reminds me, I owe you an apology."

"For what?" He glanced at her, distracted from the paint cans and brushes.

"You were right about Shawna. She was holding something back, trying to be a tough soldier instead of a little girl."

"What happened? She's all right, isn't she?"

That instant concern for her children told her more about his feelings than anything else could. Her heart twisted. If only he could see that his caring and concern were more important than any physical strength.

"She's fine now." Her voice choked a little. "It wasn't the problem that was so bad—just her way of dealing with it. If she hadn't fallen out of the tree, I'm not sure how long it would have taken me to realize what was going on."

"If you're trying to make me feel better about her getting hurt—"

"No. I'm trying to tell you that you were right about Shawna." She wanted to touch him and didn't dare. "You saw what was going on with her and I was blind to it. That's a little humiliating for a mother, you know."

He stood, shoving the stool away and taking his canes, and she suspected he was using the movement to cover the emotion that gripped him. If he would just admit what he was feeling, but he wouldn't.

"You shouldn't think that," he said finally. "You're a good mother. Those two kids couldn't ask for better. As far as any insight I might have, well, sometimes the person on the outside sees more. That's all."

The person on the outside. He was reiterating that, just in case she hadn't gotten it already.

She had to clear her throat before she could speak. "Well, thank you, in any event. For the wisdom and for the car. We've all benefited from the past month."

That sounded like an ending. Judging from Luke's expression, it was.

He moved slightly, his gaze evading hers. "It's been a good month, even if I haven't acted that way all the time. You've brought me a lot farther than I expected to come, and I'm grateful."

"I sense a 'but' coming." It took an effort to keep the smile planted on her face.

"I think I've made enough progress, thanks to you, that I'd be comfortable going to the clinic for my regular therapy sessions in addition to the pool. I've already spoken to the director about it. He's going to set something up."

She'd known it was coming. It was the natural progress of things. She wanted him to stand on his own, without her. So why did it have to hurt this much?

She mastered her emotions enough to speak. "I see. Did you also ask for a new therapist?"

"No! I didn't say anything that would reflect badly on you. Do you think I'd do that, after everything you've done for me?"

She couldn't stop the tears that welled in her eyes. She shouldn't let him see, but it was too late. He made some inarticulate sound and reached out to wipe the tear from her cheek. She swayed toward him, drawn to the warmth and caring that seemed to flow from him.

He pulled back, the movement sharp and jerky, as if it weren't quite under control. He took a long breath, so deep that she could see the movement of his chest.

"I'm sorry..." she began.

"Don't be." He sounded almost angry. "It's not your fault or mine. We're attracted to each other. We can't control what we feel, but we can control what we do. I was wrong to think this could go anywhere. The issue isn't that you're my therapist. It's that I could never be a father to your kids, and you shouldn't settle for anything less."

Pain shivered through her. Here was the honesty she'd wanted, but it didn't do her any good. He was the only one who could change his attitude, and she didn't think he ever would.

Michael's footsteps thudded on the porch and the screen door banged open. Luke turned, relieved to look away from the hurt in Mary Kate's face—pain he'd put there. He fought to tamp down an unreasonable rush of anger, so that the look he showed Michael wouldn't scare the kid.

"Luke, Luke!" Michael raced into the workroom and hurtled himself at Luke. "Come quick. There's a man outside with a car for you."

"A car?" Obviously a mistake of some sort, but at least dealing with it would get him away from Mary Kate and the constant reminder of what he couldn't have. "All right, tell him I'm coming."

He followed Michael out, aware of Mary Kate's movement behind him. When he reached the back porch he halted, staring.

There was a car in the driveway, a fairly new sedan. Behind it a truck had pulled in, and he didn't need to read the lettering on the side to know what it said. *Marino Motors.*

Someone got out of the sedan, closing the door and turning. His father.

Emotions tumbled through him. He headed for the driveway, reminding himself that Michael stood there, looking on, his eyes wide. He'd have to control himself. He couldn't say any of the things he wanted to say in front of the boy.

He stalked toward his father, wielding the canes as if they were weapons. His father stood there at the edge of the grass, watching him come. Arrogant, always expecting other people to come to him. Nothing had changed.

He came to a halt a few feet away, reminding himself again of Michael's presence, and glanced at his father. "What are you doing here?"

"I came to see you." His frown echoed Luke's. "If you recall, I've been trying to talk with you since you got back, but you wouldn't cooperate."

"It's a few years too late for that." *Why didn't you come around when I needed you, when I looked up at every knock on the door, hoping it was you?*

"Can't you let the past go?" He shook his head. "Silly question. Of course you can't. All right, I'll just say what I came to say and then I'll leave."

You're good at that, Dad. Leaving is what you do best.

His father hesitated, and for an instant Luke almost thought he was ill at ease. But that couldn't be. His father was always the most self-assured person he'd ever known.

He gestured toward the car. "I had it fitted up with hand controls after I talked to the clinic director about what you might need. It's for you."

Luke couldn't have been more shocked if his father had dropped a helicopter in his driveway. He shook his head, trying not to look at the car. "I don't want it. I don't want anything from you."

"You've made that clear enough. But like it or not, you need this. Ask her." His father jerked his head toward the porch, and Luke realized that Mary Kate was standing there. Listening. "She's the therapist. She'll tell you. This is a way for you to be independent."

"I said I don't want it. You don't listen." Always sure he was right—that was his father. If he had kids, he'd treat them differently. But he'd never have kids, so he wouldn't get the chance.

"I've listened." His father's face darkened. "I've tried to respect your privacy, but if my son needs something I can provide, I'm going to do it. I don't expect this to make us friends. I just want a chance to give you something and not have to hide it."

"What are you talking about?" He took a step toward his father. "Hiding what?"

"Nothing." He shot a quick glance at Mary Kate and shook his head. "I didn't mean anything. Just take the stupid car."

Luke looked from his father to Mary Kate, and it all started adding up—all the equipment, the endless hours she put in, the way the clinic director seemed so eager to give him anything he wanted.

Fury tightened every muscle. "You've been paying for my therapy."

"Not all of it." He held out a hand in a placating gesture. "Just the extra things the army didn't cover."

"I'll pay you back. Now take the car and get out of here."

"I don't want to be paid back. I won't take it." His father's anger rose to match his. "And the car is yours. The keys and the title are on the front seat. Keep it, sell it, turn it into scrap metal for all I care. But I'm not taking it back." He spun and strode off toward the waiting truck, and in a moment it had pulled out of the driveway and was speeding down the quiet street.

All the words he hadn't had a chance to shout pressed against his throat, wanting to come out. Anger still boiled in his veins, with nowhere to go.

He turned on Mary Kate. "You knew." He threw the words at her. "You knew, and you never said a word. How could you do that to me?"

Mary Kate's freckles stood out against white skin and her eyes blazed. She bent over Michael, patting his shoulder.

"I want you to go on over to Grammy's house, okay? I'll be there in a little bit, after I talk with Luke."

"But my car—"

"Michael, enough. You know you can't take the car until it's dry. Go on, now. Tell Grammy I'll be there soon."

Michael pouted, but clearly he knew argument would do no good. "Bye, Luke. I'll see you later, okay?"

He managed to nod. "Later."

Michael started off down the street. He waited until he thought the boy was safely out of earshot before he opened his mouth. "I want—"

Mary Kate turned toward the house. "I think you've treated the neighbors to enough of a display for one day. Let's go inside." And she walked away.

Chapter Fifteen

❧

It was obvious that they were going to have a fight about this. Mary Kate used the moments it took to walk into the house for some intensive prayer.

I'm not sure how to handle this, Lord. Please, give me the right words.

Luke had barely cleared the kitchen door when he slammed it, the sound echoing through the empty house. He leaned toward her, holding the twin canes so tightly that his fingers were white.

"You knew about this. You knew, and you didn't tell me."

She winced inwardly at the anger in his voice, but she managed to keep her face calm. "Yes, I knew. My supervisor told me when he assigned me to the case that your father wanted to pay for anything you needed."

"You know how I feel about him." A vein throbbed at Luke's temple.

"I do, and I'm sorry. For both of you. Can't you see that, Luke? But my supervisor gave me a direct order. I didn't have a choice."

"We always have a choice. You chose to lie."

The careful control she'd been keeping on her emotions slipped. "I did not lie to you. Stop trying to bully me, Luke. You should know me well enough to know that's not going to work."

He glared at her for another moment and then the tension that gripped his whole body seemed to ease a fraction. "No. Nobody was ever able to bully Mary Kate Flanagan."

"You were one of my first clients." She could breathe again, could think about how she might get through to Luke. "Are you really saying that I should have thrown away the job that supports my children for the sake of telling you something you didn't want to hear? Because that's what it comes down to. I'm on probation and if I'd made a mistake like that, I'd be gone."

He clamped his lips tight, as if to hold back

words he couldn't say. Finally he shook his head. "I suppose not. But that doesn't make me feel very kindly toward your boss."

"He's trying to run a clinic that serves every client well." She might not agree with the man, but she had to give him that. "He saw an opportunity to provide the best possible care for you and he took it. After all, it's not as if you were coming to the clinic and being a model patient."

"You've got me there." He stalked to the table, jerked out a chair and sat down. "All right. I can't be mad at you and I can't be mad at your boss. Can I at least resent my father's actions in going behind my back?"

She slid into the seat opposite him, relieved that the storm seemed to be over. "I suppose I can't prevent that. But you have to admit that he was trying to make amends, even if he went about it badly."

"It's too late for amends." His face tightened again. "He should have done it while my mother was still alive. She might have forgiven him. I can't."

The things her mother had told her about Ruth and Phillip Marino flickered through her mind. She'd have to tread carefully if she were going to say anything at all about his parents.

"I've always thought that no one, probably even a son or daughter, ever really knows what's going on inside someone else's marriage."

He shrugged, not seeming to get what she was trying so carefully to say. "I'll have to get someone to haul that car back to the dealership."

"Is that really necessary? You heard what your father said. He doesn't expect the car to make things right between you."

"Good. Because it won't."

Not as long as you're so determined to think the worst of him. Saying that would hardly help matters.

She tried for a persuasive tone. "Would it be so bad to keep the car, just until you're ready to move to an automatic? Then you could donate it to someone else who needs it."

"I don't want anything to do with that car." A muscle twitched in his jaw, emphasizing the words.

"But, Luke—"

His palm slapped down on the tabletop. "Leave it, Mary Kate. I'm not taking anything from him. That car is nothing to me but a symbol of everything that's wrong between us."

Her own frustration mounted again, pounding at her temples like a migraine. "Fine. I'll leave it alone, even if I do think you're being pigheaded about the whole thing."

They were coming to an end, weren't they? And they'd returned, full circle, to where they'd been that first day—frustrated and annoyed, glaring at each other across a chasm of differences that separated them.

"My relationship with my father doesn't concern you." He turned his face away, as if to dismiss her from his sight.

"No. I guess not." She stood, defeat weighing heavily on her shoulders. "If you're too stubborn to leave the past behind, there's nothing I can do about it."

His face swung back, tight and angry. "Is that what you're doing? Leaving the past behind?"

"Maybe I haven't always been successful, but I'm trying." Tears pricked behind her eyes, but she wouldn't let them flow. "At least I'm coming to terms with the bad things that have happened to me, instead of taking pleasure in nursing a grudge for the rest of my life."

She turned and walked out quickly, before he could say anything in response, because if she didn't, she wouldn't be able to hold back the tears.

* * *

Luke stared out the living-room window at the flags that fluttered from every house along the street. It was Memorial Day, and he'd neglected to put the flag out. He'd nearly forgotten what day it was—something about the absence of Mary Kate from his life seemed to have screwed up his internal calendar. He'd gotten used to arranging his routine around her visits.

Well, that was over now, and best for everyone.

I did the right thing, didn't I? The voice of prayer, rusty from disuse, was beginning to come back to him. *I can't ever be a father figure to her children, so I shouldn't open up the possibility of hurt.*

The trouble was that they'd already been hurt—he, and Mary Kate and maybe even the children. He'd become a part of their lives, like it or not, and now he'd cut them off.

Because I had to. He couldn't take care of them, and any relationship with Mary Kate had to include her kids. He had to believe that he was right in this.

The flag should be in the kitchen broom closet. That was where his mother had always kept it, and he certainly hadn't done any rearranging since he'd been home. He headed toward the closet, but stopped before he reached the door at the thud of feet on the back porch.

Michael's face appeared, pressed against the screen. "Luke? Are you home?"

Irrational, to feel so happy to see the kid. "Sure I am. Come in." Caution intervened. "Do you have permission to be here?"

"Sure." Michael let the door bang behind him. "Grammy said it was okay. I'm supposed to remind you that you're still invited to the picnic with us after the parade today. You'll come, won't you?"

It was tough to fib when he was pinned by the stare of those innocent blue eyes. "I don't know yet."

Coward. Of course you know that you're not going anywhere near Mary Kate.

Better change the subject. "Tell you what. I was just going to put my flag up. Do you want to help me?"

"Sure." That seemed to be Michael's favorite word. "We put ours up this morning at our house, and then I got to help Grandpa put up his. So this will be my third flag today."

"You're getting to be a pro at it, then.

Let's take a look in the closet and see if we can find mine."

He probably should send the kid straight home, instead of spinning out his visit, but he couldn't deny that he'd missed him. The house was too quiet without the screen door slamming every now and then.

He yanked open the closet. Sure enough, there was the flag, rolled up on the upper shelf. He pulled it out and handed it to Michael, then fished around until he found the two pieces of the pole.

Michael watched as he put the pieces together, then attached the flag. "I bet you put lots of flags up when you were in the army."

"Some," he admitted. He handed the flag to the boy. "Sometimes we marched with them. How about marching that to the front door?"

He expected Michael to clown it up, but instead, face intent, the boy put the pole over his shoulder. He marched soberly to the front of the house, holding the flag with a reverence that others would do well to copy. Luke followed the small figure, his throat tight.

He opened the front door. "There should be a bracket right on the post."

Michael went first, and then he maneuvered onto the front stoop, cautious of catching the canes in the welcome mat. He took the flag Michael held out and slid it into place. Michael, standing very straight, saluted.

The small gesture grabbed Luke's heart and wouldn't let go. After an instant he followed suit, standing as much at attention as he could while gripping a cane.

"Good job," he said once he could speak. "It looks fine, doesn't it?"

"Everybody on the street has one." Michael sounded satisfied, as if that suited his sense of what was right.

"They do. Everyone's celebrating Memorial Day."

"Grandpa says that Memorial Day is to honor people who served their country. That it's okay to have fun, as long as we remember what it's for."

Heavy-duty stuff, coming from a little kid. "Your grandpa's a wise man." Luke turned back to the house. "I guess you want to pick up your car while you're here, don't you?" The car, its red paint shiny, had sat on the kitchen table most of the week, a silent reproach.

"I guess." Michael trailed him back to the kitchen. He leaned against the table. "It looks nice, doesn't it?"

Something in the boy's tone alerted Luke

that this wasn't a routine question. "I think it looks excellent." He sat down, drawing Michael a little closer. "What is it, buddy? You look like something's wrong."

Michael's gaze evaded his. "It's just... there's something I need to do with the car. I thought maybe you could help me with it."

What on earth... "If I can, I will. Why don't you tell me about it?"

He nodded. "I don't want the car for the school project. I want to take it to the cemetery and put it on my daddy's grave." There were no tears in Michael's eyes. He said the words with perfect calm.

"I see." He was the one having trouble with tears. "Can you tell me why?"

"We were going to make the car together, and we couldn't, 'cause he got sick. I want to show Daddy that I did it, just like he would want me to."

Mary Kate would have a fit if she heard him try to respond to that, but what else could he do? He put his arm around the boy.

"Michael, you know your daddy's not there at the cemetery, not really. He's in Heaven with Jesus."

"I know. But today everybody will put flowers and flags on the graves 'cause it's

Memorial Day. Mom and Grammy already went and did that. But I wanted to have something special to put on my daddy's grave." His lip trembled a little. "I would've done it last year, but I couldn't finish the car by myself."

Please, Lord, let me say the right thing.

"Why didn't you tell your mommy that? You could have taken it when they went."

"I thought it would make her sad." Michael turned, giving him the full effect of his wide-eyed stare. "I thought you could take me."

There were a thousand reasons he couldn't and shouldn't do that, but trying to frame them in a way that a child could understand made him realize that all the reasons were cop-outs. There was only one genuine one.

"If that's what you want, I'll take you." It looked as if the unwelcome gift from his father was going to see some use after all. "But we have to call your mommy first and make sure it's okay. I can't take you anywhere unless she says so. All right?"

Michael thought it over for a moment, and then he nodded. "Okay." He leaned against Luke's arm. "It'll be okay if you tell her. You'll know what to say so she won't be sad."

Michael had a lot more faith in him than

he had in himself. He reached for the phone, hoping he could talk around the stranglehold the kid had on his heart.

"Whose cell phone is that?" Mary Kate's sister, Terry, glanced around the kitchen, which was crowded with Flanagan females putting together the Memorial Day picnic.

"Mine." Mary Kate dropped the spoon she'd been using to stir potato salad and wiped her hands on the closest dish towel. She snatched her handbag off the stool and pulled the phone out. "Hello?"

Silence for a moment, just long enough to make her nervous.

"Mary Kate. It's Luke."

"Luke." The clatter in the kitchen had stopped, as everyone looked at her and then looked away, trying not to show their interest. She pushed out the kitchen door to the back porch. "I didn't expect to hear from you today."

Or anytime. He'd followed through on his plan to start therapy at the clinic, and somehow he always managed to come when she was off duty. Well, that hadn't been a surprise, had it? She'd known what he intended.

"No, I—" He actually sounded unsure of himself. "Did you know that Michael is here?"

"Mom said she sent him over to remind you of the picnic." And Mom hadn't asked her first, probably afraid the answer would be no.

"He told me that." Luke's voice seemed to deepen. "But he had another reason for coming over today."

"Another reason?" She walked to the railing, staring down at the irises blooming along the edge of Mom's flower bed like so many cream, yellow and purple flags. "I suppose he wanted to pick up his car."

She would not let herself be affected by the sound of Luke's voice. She was over him. She was.

"Not exactly. He wants me to help him with something. To take the car to the cemetery and put it with the flowers on his father's grave."

She couldn't possibly speak. But she had to. "He told you that?"

"Yes." His voice softened to a low murmur in her ear. "I'm sorry this is coming from me. I'm probably the last person you want to hear it from."

"It's...it's all right." She struggled to keep the tears from sounding in her voice. "I don't understand. If he wanted to do that, why didn't he go with us this morning?"

Instead of turning to you. Luke didn't want to be responsible for her kids, but that was exactly what he was doing. Did he even realize that?

"He said he didn't want to make you sad."

It hurt just as much now as it had the first time she'd heard it from Michael, when he'd tried to explain why he hadn't told her about the car.

"I thought we were past that. I explained…well, never mind. I'll pick him up and take him."

"He wants me to take him." Luke's frown seemed to come right through the phone line. "Look, Mary Kate, I don't really understand why Michael came to me with this, but he did. I don't figure there's much I can do for him, but if you'll let me, I can do this."

Her breath caught. "The car your father left for you."

"Funny, isn't it?" He didn't sound as if he found the situation humorous. "It even has a built-in kid's booster seat in the back."

No, it didn't feel funny. It felt meant. But she didn't suppose he'd see it that way. She was having enough trouble with that herself.

Giving this over to Luke went against everything she'd told herself since Kenny got sick—that she had to be the strong one, that she had to be everything to her kids, that no one else could do it for her.

Is that why, Father? Have You used Luke to bring me to knowing that I can't do it all?

Her heart twisted with the added pain that it was Luke, of all people. Luke, who was trying so hard to shut them out of his life.

He was waiting for her answer, and there was only one thing she could say, as hard as it was.

"All right. If that's what Michael wants." Questions battered at her heart, but she didn't suppose Luke could answer any of them.

"Mary Kate…" He sighed, as if he couldn't find the words. "Look, just don't worry so much."

"Can't help it. It comes with the territory." She pressed the phone hard against her ear. "I won't intrude, but I'm driving over to the cemetery. I'll park down the hill a bit so… well, so you can signal me if he wants me."

"Will do." He clicked off.

He hung up so that he could go and make this pilgrimage with her child. For an instant everything in her rebelled. She'd go over there, she'd talk to Michael, she'd make everything all right for him.

But she couldn't. Michael had made that clear. For whatever reason, he'd picked Luke to help him with this. She had to do the hardest thing for any mother—stand back and let her child carry a burden alone.

Chapter Sixteen

"You okay back there?" Luke glanced in the rearview mirror. Michael seemed to be sitting perfectly at ease in the booster seat, the shoulder harness securing him. Luke was the one with a bad case of nerves.

Not because of the driving. That had come back surprisingly quickly and the hand controls were easy to master. Naturally he'd kept his license up to date. Much as he hated to admit it, everyone—Mary Kate, the other therapists, even his father, in a sense—had been right. Driving a car did make him feel normal again.

In control. But when he'd said that to Mary Kate, she'd responded that it was an illusion. That we were never really in control. He wasn't sure how he felt about that.

He made the turn between the cemetery gates, and his breath caught at the sight of all the flags, fluttering like waves of red, white and blue against the green. The Boy Scouts had obviously been here already this morning.

He remembered doing that when he'd been a little older than Michael was now. Even through the usual horseplay that existed wherever a bunch of boys were together, a sense of awe had come over them as they'd worked their way through the cemetery, putting flags on the grave of every veteran.

They'd crossed the cemetery from the newest to the oldest veteran's grave, standing for a while at the grave of one Jacob Taubenberger, 1758 to 1820, child of a German immigrant who'd come to Penn's Woods lured by William Penn's promises of freedom to worship. Jacob had fought at Trenton and lived through the winter at Valley Forge. Even now, the thought put a lump in Luke's throat.

But it was a more recent grave they were seeking. He turned up the lane that led to the new section. "Do you know where we're going, Michael?"

Michael leaned forward, pointing. "Right up there, behind the little house."

The little house was a mausoleum, but he didn't suppose that was in the child's vocabulary. He pulled to the side where Michael indicated and turned off the engine.

Once out of the car, Michael walked surely across the grass, carrying the model car in both hands like an offering. Luke followed, grateful that the grass had obviously been cut recently enough that it didn't give him much trouble. Flowers blossomed in front of gray stones—geraniums, marigolds, a few mums.

Michael stopped, squatting down. He reached out to touch the red and white geraniums his mother and grandmother had planted.

Luke lowered himself to the grass next to the boy, not sure what, if anything, he should say.

I know I haven't turned to You the way I should, Father, but I am now. I don't know what Michael needs from me today, but please, please keep me from letting him down.

The words from an old gospel hymn they'd sung at worship yesterday rang in his mind. *The Lord will make a way somehow.* That was what he had to lean on. The thought blossomed in his mind. Not his own strength.

The Lord would make a way for him to help Michael today.

Michael looked down at the car, running his finger along the racing stripe they'd painted, bright against the red. Then he nestled it among the flowers. He sat back on his heels, looking at it.

"I wish my daddy could see it." He leaned against Luke, as if wanting to feel his touch. "Do you think he can?"

Luke didn't know the theological answer to that, but he knew what was in his heart. "Yes, I think he can." He put his hand on Michael's shoulder. "I think people who loved us never stop loving us, even if they're not with us anymore."

He paused, feeling—well, a little confused. His father had loved him once, hadn't he? And he'd loved his father with all a child's heart and understanding. Was that now broken beyond repair?

"I thought maybe Daddy was disappointed that I didn't finish the car."

The words took Luke's breath away for an instant. This was it, then, the thing that lay deep in the child's heart—the fear that he'd somehow let down the person whose approval he needed most in the world.

He knew how that felt, didn't he? A boy turned to his mother for comfort, hugs, encouragement. He turned to his father for approval, for the affirmation that he was turning into the right kind of man. That was what he'd wanted when he'd held out his first stumbling efforts at woodworking, longing for his father's approval.

Please, give me the words.

"You know, Michael, I believe that you never let your daddy down. Maybe sometimes he was tired, or impatient, but he never felt that you let him down." His throat choked and he fought to speak over it. "Now he's not sick anymore and he's never tired or rushed. And he loves you and is proud of you, always."

Michael looked up in his face as he said the words, his small face intent. Looking at him as if he had the answers. As if it was Luke's approval that he needed right now.

The feeling overwhelmed him. He'd never intended to be responsible for another living soul, but somehow, without even knowing it, he'd become responsible in some small way for helping Michael.

He cleared his throat. "I knew your daddy for a long time. He was a good, strong, honorable man, the kind of person you could trust with your life. You're going to grow up to be just like him."

Those blue eyes stared into his for another long moment. Then Michael nodded. He flung himself against Luke, arms around his neck. "I love you, Luke."

Luke held him tight, his heart full. "I love you, too." He hugged the boy fiercely and kissed the top of his bright head. "Know what? Your mom is waiting down the road a little way. How about we go to meet her?"

Michael scrambled to his feet and wiped his face with the backs of his hands. "Okay." He moved closer to Luke. "You can hold on to my shoulder to get up."

This kid was pummeling his heart until it was going to be as soft as a fistful of feathers. He put one hand on the small shoulder, letting the cane take most of his weight, and struggled to his feet.

Once he'd gained his balance, he waved toward Mary Kate's car. The door opened so quickly that it was obvious her hand had already been on the handle. She started toward them as they moved toward her. The breeze on the hilltop ruffled her mahogany curls as it ruffled the flags on the graves.

She reached them, and he realized she was

looking to him for guidance on how to react. He nodded, managing a smile.

"Everything's okay. Michael did what he needed to do."

"That's good." She gave her son a quick hug, probably not as tight as she'd like it to be.

His heart twisted. Mary Kate tried so hard, gave so much. He wanted to give her something in return, to hold something out to her in both hands, the way Michael had carried the car as a gift to his father.

"Well, I guess we should get going." She shoved her hair back with both hands. "We want to find a good spot to watch the parade."

He knew, then, what he could give her. He looked across the peaceful green hillside, alive with the pristine flags that seemed so much a part of it that they might have grown there.

Each flag marked sacrifice. Other people had given so much, had suffered and wept and died. Who was he to act as if his injuries were so much greater than theirs, or to be embarrassed to have people see him as he was now?

He straightened his shoulders, his hand resting lightly on Michael's head. "Right. I'd better hurry if I'm going to have time to get into my uniform and join the other veterans for the parade."

Fierce joy blossomed on Mary Kate's face at his words, going straight to his heart. He'd been right. His heart was never going to be the same.

Mary Kate set a container of chocolate cupcakes on the picnic table and stood back a step to let a horde of little Flanagans at them. The adults might be happier with the strawberry and rhubarb pies her mother had brought, but nothing beat chocolate cupcakes for kids.

The Flanagans had claimed three picnic tables under one of the huge old oaks in the park, but even so they'd had to overflow onto lawn chairs and blankets. She glanced across the crowd, her gaze drawn irresistibly to the tall figure in uniform who stood at the edge of the group.

Luke was talking to someone, but it wasn't one of her brothers. Phillip Marino stood next to his son. They both looked a bit stiff, a bit wary, but at least they were talking. Even as she watched, Phil reached out to pat Luke's arm awkwardly. And Luke didn't pull away.

Thank You, Lord. If Luke has begun to let go of his resentment toward his father, he really is healing.

Phil walked off toward another pavilion, looking as if a weight had been lifted from his shoulders. And Luke came toward her.

He stopped, glancing around at the swarm of Flanagans. "Much as I like your family, do you think we could find a spot that's a little more private?"

Her heart seemed to be fluttering up in her throat. She nodded toward a bench that sat a little apart, half hidden by a clump of rhodo-dendrons covered in purple blooms. They walked to it side by side, not speaking.

Luke lowered himself to the bench, bracing one hand against its back.

She sat next to him. "Sure you haven't been overdoing it a little?"

"Don't fuss, Mary Kate." There was a gleam of laughter in his eyes.

"I can't help it," she said. "You know that."

"Yes, I do. It's one of the things I love about you."

Her breath caught. It was an expression, that was all. Luke wasn't, couldn't be, talking about love.

"Don't do that," he said softly. His hand

closed over hers. "You're telling yourself I don't mean that, aren't you?"

She nodded. She couldn't find something to say if her life depended on it.

"Well, stop it." His tone was deep with mock severity. "I blew this once before, and I don't want to blow it this time. I love you, Mary Kate Flanagan Donnelly. I'm not sure what we're going to do about it, but I'm done fighting it. I love you."

She managed to meet his eyes, and the love she saw shining there pierced her heart and took away all her defenses. "I still have two kids, you know. And a very managing disposition. Nothing has changed."

"Everything has changed." He corrected her gently. "When Michael turned to me today, when you were able to trust me with him, when I was able to give him what he needed, everything changed. I saw how stupid I've been."

She grasped his hand, letting herself cling to it. Letting herself hope. "Not stupid. Just hurting."

"That, too." He looked down at their entwined hands, his expression serious. "Ever since I was wounded, the only thing I thought I could settle for was to be whole again. Today I realized there's more than one way of being whole."

Thank You, Lord. Thank You.

"I'm glad." She had to whisper the words to get them out.

He turned on the bench so that he was facing her. "I don't know how much more I'm going to get back. And I don't know what I'm going to be doing for the rest of my working life." His smile flickered, touching her heart. "But if you're willing to take a chance on a future with a lot of question marks…"

She touched his face, feeling the warmth that radiated from him moving through her fingertips, warming her, too. "I know everything I need to know about your future. I know that you're a good, strong, caring man who will always do the right thing. I can't ask for more than that."

All the doubts she'd been harboring seemed to be floating away on the warm breeze. She loved Kenny, but Kenny was gone and she knew in her heart he didn't begrudge her this happiness. As for the children—well, Luke had already shown that he had what it took to be a father. He just hadn't been ready to admit it until now.

She lifted her face toward his, a smile trembling on her lips. "I love you, Luke Marino. Now and always."

Epilogue

"Happy anniversary, Grammy." Michael planted a kiss on Siobhan's cheek and raced away again to join his cousins in a noisy game that seemed to involve running wildly around the backyard.

Siobhan smiled, leaning back in the lawn chair. It didn't matter how noisy the grandkids were today, since the whole neighborhood seemed to be in the Flanagan backyard, joining the celebration.

The banner Gabe and Seth had stretched from the treetop to the house eaves fluttered, as if it wanted to participate in the fun. *Happy 40th Anniversary to Joe and Siobhan,* it proclaimed in giant red letters.

The children had wanted to give them a huge bash at a hotel ballroom to mark the day. It had taken weeks of talking to convince them that this was what she and Joe really wanted—to be surrounded by family and friends at their own home.

How could anyone ask for a better way to celebrate forty years of marriage than this? Her gaze went to Joe first, as it always did.

Forty years. His hair was nearly white now, instead of the bright red it had once been, and he carried a few extra pounds around his middle, but when he smiled, he was still the boy who'd stolen her heart all those years ago. Time hadn't quenched the zest for life that had enchanted her then. And still did.

"Do you want anything, Mom?"

Mary Kate alighted on the seat next to her, looking as if she were ready to take off again at a moment's notice to settle a spat among the children or whip more food from the kitchen. That was Mary Kate, always taking care of everyone.

"Not a thing. Are you sure I can't help bring the desserts out?" Come to think of it, maybe Mary Kate came by that honestly.

"We have it covered." Her eldest leaned over for a quick hug. "You're queen of the day, remember?" She touched the foil-and-glitter crown the grandchildren had planted on Siobhan's head to start the party.

She nodded, content to watch as Mary Kate headed back to the kitchen, detouring a little to say a word to her new husband. Luke still leaned on a single cane, but he was miles better than he'd been a year ago. He seemed to be thriving on marriage, instant fatherhood to Mary Kate's two children and his new job as a juvenile probation officer, where he had a chance to turn a few young lives around.

Gabe, who'd come so close after Mary Kate that it had been like having two babies, lifted three-year-old Siobhan bodily from a tangle of older cousins. Siobhan, who always thought she could do everything the older ones did, was protesting loudly, but Gabe tucked her under his arm and carted her off to his wife.

Nolie, her slim figure just starting to show the curve of her second pregnancy, was deep in conversation with Joe's niece Fiona. Since Fiona and her husband were also expecting, they were probably comparing notes.

A wave of pleasure mixed with nostalgia went through her. They were having another family baby boom. She didn't want to go back to the days when she and Joe were starting their brood, but she did love to see the family grow. She'd have to start on baby quilts for each of them soon.

The quilt she'd made for Brendan and Claire's baby was draped across the portable crib where their little Joshua slept in the shade. Little Joshua might not know it, but he was going to be the right age to be good friends with his cousin, Seth and Julie's Brian, who'd come along nine months ago to join his big brother, Davy.

Her cup really was overflowing. Her two youngest, Terry and Ryan, had found their happily-ever-after, too. Footloose Ryan had settled into marriage with an ease that surprised everyone who knew him, especially since that marriage brought a young daughter with it. Laura and Mandy had settled into the family so smoothly they might have always been there.

As for Terry's husband—Jake had probably found the Flanagan family a little overwhelming at first, but now he took part in the chaos as easily as the rest of them.

"What are you thinking about, lovely lady?" Joe bent over to give her a light kiss.

She patted his cheek. Would the kids be

embarrassed if they knew how that kiss still thrilled her? Probably. She smiled at him, loving the way his eyes warmed when they rested on her.

"Just thinking how much God has blessed us." She took his hand, holding it against her cheek. "Children, grandchildren, friends, family all here to celebrate with us. I couldn't ask for anything better."

He nodded, his blue eyes, still bright after all these years, suddenly thoughtful. "We've hit some storms along the way, but He's always seen us through." He smiled suddenly. "You know I'm not one to quote Bible verses easily, but there's one that's been floating around my heart a lot today."

She smiled. "I think I know what it is, because it's been in my heart, too."

"You always could read me like a book, couldn't you?" A sheen of tears glinted suddenly in his eyes. "Still, I guess it's a pretty obvious verse for the Flanagan family." He hesitated for a moment, and then said the words that were in both their hearts.

"'As for me and my family, we will follow the Lord.'"

* * * * *

Watch for Marta Perry's next novel,
HIDE IN PLAIN SIGHT,
the first story in the exciting new miniseries
THE THREE SISTERS INN.
Danger awaits the Hampton sisters in
quiet Amish Country.
On sale in August 2007 from
Steeple Hill Love Inspired Suspense.

Dear Reader,

Thank you for picking up this final book in the Flanagan family story. I hope you enjoyed visiting with old friends and meeting new ones, and that you'll feel the series came to a satisfying conclusion. It's never easy for an author to say goodbye to characters, especially ones I know as well as these.

Mary Kate Flanagan Donnelly has appeared in all the books, so it was high time she had a story of her own. Her story would have been much more difficult to write without the professional knowledge of my physical therapist niece, Pam Johnson, who shared her experience with me. Any mistakes are strictly my own!

I hope you'll let me know how you felt about this story. I'd love to hear from you, and you can write to me at Steeple Hill Books, 233 Broadway, Suite 1001, New York, NY 10279; e-mail me at marta@martaperry.com or visit me on the Web at www.martaperry.com.

Blessings,

Marta Perry

QUESTIONS FOR DISCUSSION

1. What qualities in Mary Kate make her a good physical therapist? Do you think her innate nurturing instincts work for her or against her?

2. Luke feels that his injuries will keep him from ever being useful again. Do you sympathize with his feelings, even if you may not approve of his reactions?

3. Mary Kate has a particularly close relationship with her mother, yet she doesn't want to rely on her too much. Do you empathize with her conflicting feelings about her mother, as she struggles with being a single parent?

4. The struggle to cope with loss is central to this story, as Mary Kate tries to cope with the loss of her husband and Luke with the loss of his physical prowess. Have you ever gone through a similar struggle? What helped you the most?

5. Mary Kate comes to feel that God leads her to a place where she can help Luke. Have you ever felt that God has led you to a particular place or situation?

6. Mary Kate also finds that God has something to teach her, as the person she helps ends up helping her. Have you found that to be true in your life?

7. Luke tries to block everyone out of his life, but Mary Kate's son, Michael, is able to find the chink in Luke's armor. What quality does the child have that allows him to do something like that?

8. In the scriptural theme, we see that Christ has come to bind up all wounds. In what way has Christ worked in your life to bind up your wounds?

9. Luke struggles with his relationship with his father, asking why it would be right to forgive someone who's betrayed a child. How would you answer him?

10. If you've read all seven of the Flanagan books, you must feel that you know the family well. What qualities do you think enable them to overcome difficulties and come out with their peace and faith intact?

HEARTWARMING INSPIRATIONAL ROMANCE

Contemporary,
inspirational romances
with Christian characters
·facing the challenges
of life and love
in today's world.

**NOW AVAILABLE IN REGULAR
AND LARGER-PRINT FORMATS.**

Steeple
Hill®

For exciting stories that reflect traditional values,
visit:
www.steeplehillbooks.com

Love Inspired®

SUSPENSE
RIVETING INSPIRATIONAL ROMANCE

Watch for our new series of
edge-of-your-seat suspense novels.
These contemporary tales
of intrigue and romance
feature Christian characters
facing challenges to their faith...
and their lives!

NOW AVAILABLE IN REGULAR
AND LARGER-PRINT FORMATS.

Steeple
Hill®

Visit:
www.steeplehillbooks.com